Hearts in Harmony

A Bindarra Creek Christmas in July Romance

Annie Seaton

This book is a work of fiction. Names, characters, places, magazines and incidents are the product of the author's imagination or are used fictitiously. Any resemblance to actual events, locales, or persons, living or dead, is coincidental.

Chapter One

Early April

Beth Curtis gripped the steering wheel tightly when the sign for Bindarra Creek—population 2,988—appeared ahead on the left. The tension in her shoulders had been building for the last fifty kilometres, and her neck was aching. She'd driven non-stop from Sydney up the New England Highway, stopping once for petrol, a takeaway egg and lettuce sandwich, and a quick bathroom break in Tamworth. The car was loaded with the boxes, suitcases, and guitar that represented her new life.

A life without David.

"First stop, coffee," she muttered to herself, slowing down as the main street came into view.

Beth rolled down the window, catching her breath as dry, warm air rushed into the car. She snatched a glance at the map on her phone, grateful for the directions she'd committed to memory in case she lost reception. Everything in the country was an unknown to her. The furthest she'd ever been from Sydney was a weekend trip to Mudgee when she was at uni.

The town itself was a surprise. She'd pictured a smaller, more dilapidated version of a Sydney suburb, but instead, the main street was quaint with its old buildings and wide verandas. Bright hanging flower baskets provided a splash of colour against some of the buildings.

The tension in her shoulders eased slightly. Perhaps it wouldn't be so bad, after all. It wasn't as if she'd had a choice anyway. The teaching position at Bindarra Creek High School had been her only offer after—well, after everything. Coming to start at a new school in the country at the beginning of term two was going to be hard enough without settling into a whole new town. But the thought of staying in Sydney, where memories of David lurked on every corner, had been unbearable.

"Coffee," she said aloud. "Coffee, then keys to the house."

Her gaze settled on a café ahead, and she slowed. A mud-stained four-wheel drive pulled out in front of her, and she quickly slipped her small sedan into the space. She pulled out a brush from her handbag and checked her reflection in the rear-view mirror before she took the brush to her unruly curls. No matter what she did, her hair always seemed to spring into a mess. Dark circles under her eyes matched her dark hair, contrasting with her fair skin.

Beth put the hairbrush away, thought about lipstick briefly, and shrugged. It wasn't as though she was going to see anyone she knew.

Picking up her handbag, she pushed open the car door and headed to the café she'd spotted. Her eyes widened at the Greek-style columns beneath a blue and white awning. The bell above the café door jangled as she stepped inside, and the warmth enveloped her immediately. Greek and Australian flags hung along freshly painted blue and white walls, making the red seats in the booths along the far wall stand out. Free-standing tables and chairs filled the space between booths and the counter.

The rich aroma of coffee mingled with the enticing smell of something baking. Beth's stomach grumbled loudly, and embarrassment warmed her already rosy cheeks. There was a sudden lull in conversation as several heads turned to examine the newcomer.

"Large flat white, please," Beth asked the woman behind the counter. "Extra shot."

"Long drive?" The quiet voice came from behind her.

Beth turned to see a tall woman waiting to be served. Long, slightly curly auburn hair caught the afternoon sun. Her hazel eyes held interest, and her smile was friendly.

"Yes, from Sydney," Beth confirmed, pulling out her wallet.

"Ah, city girl? Just a coffee stop?"

Beth hesitated. "Actually, I'm moving here. I'm the new music teacher at the high school."

The woman's smile widened.

"Oh, you're Miss Curtis! We've been expecting you. I'm Claire McGregor. My daughter Meg has been so excited since she heard we were finally getting a music teacher. She desperately wants to learn to play the piano." Claire shook her head. "We don't know where that comes from; neither my husband nor I are the least bit musical."

"Is she at the high school?"

"No, Megan's only six, but she already knows her own mind. And it'll be good to see her learn an instrument."

The woman behind the counter handed Beth her takeaway coffee. "Enjoy. And welcome to Bindarra Creek, Miss Curtis. Claire, you'll have to introduce her to Angus."

Beth knew she must have looked surprised when Claire moved closer and lowered her voice.

"First rule of small towns," she said with a wink. "Everyone knows everyone. You'll get your chance to meet us all before long. I'm sure you'll have a lot to do with the Christmas festivities. Both schools are going to be involved, as well as all the service clubs and organisations in town."

"Christmas?" Beth frowned. Christmas was three terms away.

"Christmas in July. I've just come from a committee meeting."

"Oh. Maybe. Anyway, lovely meeting you, Claire. I must go. I have a lot to do this afternoon."

Claire nodded. "I'm sure we'll meet again soon. There's bound to be a welcome function for you."

Beth stepped back out onto the street, coffee in hand, already thinking of ways she could politely decline involvement in any Christmas festivities or welcome dinners. She was going to keep a low profile in Bindarra Creek. She'd go to school, focus on her new classes, and have a professional relationship with her colleagues. She had vowed to keep to herself and not get into personal discussions about what brought her to Bindarra Creek.

"Music' would be her stock answer.

It still hurt too much to talk about her real reason for fleeing Sydney, the school she loved, and her apartment.

The real estate agency was easy to find, and Beth was about to push the door open when it swung outwards unexpectedly, and she collided with a woman rushing out, nearly spilling her coffee down both of them.

"I'm so sorry!" they exclaimed simultaneously, and then laughed.

The woman she'd bumped into was striking—tall and willowy with golden-blonde hair cut in a stylish bob.

"My fault entirely," the woman said, her smile warm and open. "I was in such a rush, I wasn't looking where I was going."

"No harm done," Beth assured her, relieved

that her coffee had survived.

"You're new in town," the woman tilted her head slightly as she studied Beth. It wasn't a question.

Beth smiled. "Is it that obvious?"

"New faces stand out. Plus," she added with a grin, "everyone who's been here more than five minutes knows not to stand directly in front of that door. There's a blind spot, and Laurie has a habit of bursting through it like he's making a grand entrance."

Beth laughed despite herself, feeling some of the tension ease from her shoulders. "I'm Beth Curtis. I've just arrived."

"Violet Valentine," the woman replied, offering her hand. "I was new to town last year. But don't worry, this is a fabulous place to live. Bindarra Creek will take you into its fold."

Beth tried to keep her expression pleasant; she didn't want to be taken into any fold. "What brought you to Bindarra Creek?"

"A fresh start," Violet said, something flickering behind her eyes before her smile returned. "I'm an equine vet at Blue Orchard Park. What brings you to town?"

"I'm the new music teacher at the high

school," Beth explained, the phrase becoming more real each time she said it aloud.

"Welcome." Violet glanced at her watch. "Look, I've got to get back to the stud now—mare about to foal—but would you like to have coffee sometime? I know what it's like to be new in a close-knit town."

The invitation was so unexpected and welcome that a surprising prick of tears stung her eyes. She blinked them away quickly. "I'd like that."

They exchanged phone numbers, and Beth found herself smiling genuinely for what felt like the first time in months.

So much for keeping to myself.

"Oh, and fair warning," Violet added as she turned to go, "everyone knows everything here. By dinnertime, half the town will know you're the new music teacher, where you're living, what sort of coffee you drink, and they'll be speculating about why you chose Bindarra Creek."

Beth's smile faltered. "Great."

"Don't worry," Violet said, touching her arm lightly. "Most of it's harmless. They're good people, just interested." She lowered her voice conspiratorially. "Have you heard about our Christmas in July? It's a whole month of festivities."

"Yes, I've heard already," Beth said with a small grimace.

"I know, right? Something about tourism and community spirit. I've already been roped into helping somehow." Violet rolled her eyes good-naturedly. "You probably will be, too, especially being a music teacher. They'll be after you to organise carols or something."

That familiar anxiety twisted in her stomach. Public performances. David's voice echoed in her head: *You embarrass me, Beth. You're too rigid. No wonder you never made it as a performer.*

"Anyway," Violet continued, oblivious to Beth's sudden discomfort, "Laurie's waiting for you. He has your keys. The cottage is small but sweet—I considered it briefly before I decided to stay with Joe. But that's a story for over coffee. And between you and me, I've heard the hot water system is temperamental. Run the kitchen sink for a minute before you try the shower."

Beth blinked. "How do you know which

cottage—"

"It's a small town," Violet reminded her with a smile. "Only one rental available right now, and Laurie mentioned the new teacher was arriving today." She glanced at her watch again. "I have to dash. But call me, okay? Maybe Friday for that coffee?"

"Friday," Beth confirmed, feeling slightly dazed by the whirlwind that was Violet Valentine.

With a wave, Violet hurried off down the street, her blue dress a bright splash against the faded bricks. Beth watched her go, a small smile playing on her lips.

Maybe this won't be so bad after all.

She turned back to the real estate office, squared her shoulders, and pushed open the door. Time to collect the keys to her new life.

A man in his fifties with a ruddy complexion and a wide smile stood up as she entered. "You must be Miss Curtis! Welcome to Bindarra Creek."

Beth bit back a laugh.

Small town indeed.

By the time she left the real estate office with keys in hand and a town map with directions to her rental arrowed in red pen, she had already been introduced to two older women—she suspected they had followed her into the real estate office—who had promptly invited her to the CWA meeting for more Christmas in July planning. Beth hadn't had time to say more than a thank you to their welcome before they left, chattering about Christmas movies and cooking classes.

"Edwina Lette and Thea Levonis," Laurie said as he handed her the keys. "Just nod and smile. Safest way not to get roped into anything."

Back in her car, Beth sat for a moment, taking deep breaths as her head whirled. She'd known that moving to a small town would mean giving up some privacy, but she hadn't expected it to be quite so immediate. Or perhaps she had, and that's why the knot in her stomach had been there from the moment she crossed into the New England region.

Tomorrow morning, she would report to Bindarra Creek High School and meet Jaclyn Rossiter face to face. Their previous conversations had been on the telephone. She would begin her new job next week on the first day of term. She would settle into her cottage and begin to build a new, quiet life focused on her teaching.

But as she started the car and followed Laurie's directions to what would be her new home, Beth made a silent promise to herself: no community plays, no Christmas carols, no public performances of any kind. And absolutely, positively, no romance.

She was here to rebuild her career and her confidence, not to put herself out there to be hurt again.

The fact that her heart had lifted briefly at the thought of having coffee with Violet was simply the relief of meeting someone else fairly new to town. Nothing more.

Chapter Two

Will Greaves woke before the alarm, as he did every morning. Setting it was a long-ingrained habit. The pre-dawn light was just beginning to soften the darkness outside his bedroom window. He lay still for a moment, listening to the familiar sounds of his farmhouse settling and creaking in the early morning chill. There was comfort in the sounds as the morning began; the same way he took comfort in the rhythm of farm life—the seasons, the stock work, the land that had been in his family for three generations.

By the time his alarm buzzed at five-thirty, Will was already dressed in worn jeans, a light flannel shirt, and his weathered Akubra hat. He moved through the kitchen, stoking the wood stove to take the edge off the autumn chill; it wouldn't be long before the first frost of the season arrived. It always made him think of his grandfather. "First frost of the season, always on the weekend before ANZAC Day, son."

And Pops had been right most years. He still missed the old fella, even though he'd been gone for five years now. At least he hadn't been around when Mum and Dad died. Brewing a strong pot of coffee and making a quick breakfast of eggs and toast took his mind off the past.

Outside, the world was painted in shades of grey and blue, the sun not yet risen over the hills that bordered Avon Downs to the east. Will's breath clouded in the crisp air as he strode towards the shearing shed where he kept his ute. The dogs, Rusty and Missy, bounded at his heels, eager for the day's work.

As the ute bumped along the rutted track, Will reviewed the day ahead. There was fencing to be done in the west paddock, a delivery of feed supplements expected around noon, and then the SES meeting at the town hall at six. The SES meeting would focus on final preparations for the winter firewood scavenging and clean-up, an annual tradition where volunteers cleared fallen timber from local properties.

Will was looking forward to the meeting. Despite the serious nature of the SES work, the meetings had a social element he enjoyed—a chance to catch up with friends and neighbours, share news, and maintain the connections that made small-town life so enjoyable.

The morning flew by, and when the delivery truck from the rural store had left, Will headed back to the house. The kitchen was warm from the sun streaming through the north-facing window. Will washed up at the sink, the cold water refreshing against his face and hands. He made a simple lunch of a thick ham and cheese sandwich with a mug of tea, eating at the large wooden table that had been Gran's pride and joy. The house was quiet around him, as it had been since the accident had taken his parents.

Will didn't mind the solitude, not really. At thirty-four, he'd grown accustomed to his own company, focusing on the needs of the farm and his animals rather than social obligations. Still, there were moments—like now, in the stillness of the kitchen—when the big old house sometimes felt empty.

His thoughts turned, as they had increasingly done in recent days, to the latest big news in town. Bindarra Creek High School was getting a new music teacher. The position had been vacant for nearly a year, and the lack of proper music education had been a frequent topic of conversation among parents at the pub and the café. Will had paid little attention to the gossip until Jon Kendall, whose wife Cleo worked part-time in the high school office, had mentioned that the new teacher was arriving from Sydney.

"City woman," Jon had said with a knowing grin over beers at the pub last week. "Single, too. Cleo's already planning to have her over for a barbecue."

Will had rolled his eyes at his friend's not-so-subtle matchmaking intentions. Jon and Cleo were happily married with two small children and seemed determined to see all their single friends similarly settled.

But despite his outward disinterest, Will was curious about the newcomer. Not that he was looking for romance—his last relationship had fizzled out when his on-again, off-again girlfriend, Melissa, had made it clear she had no intention of becoming a farmer's wife, choosing a career in Brisbane over staying in Bindarra Creek. That had been three years ago, and he hadn't been devastated, but it had left him wary of getting involved with a woman whose dreams didn't include small-town life.

Will's mobile rang, interrupting his thoughts. The screen showed Roman Taylor's name—the captain of the local SES.

"G'day, Roman," Will answered, leaning back in his chair.

"Will, mate, you're still good for tonight's meeting?"

"Course. Wouldn't miss it. We talking preparations for the winter clean-up?"

"Yeah, plus the usual bits and bobs. And..." Roman paused. "The Christmas in July committee wants to pitch the SES's involvement in the parade. They're sending a representative."

Will groaned good-naturedly. "A parade? You mean we have to decorate a float?"

"It's not a bad idea, mate. That's how they work." Roman chuckled. "Besides, it brings in tourists, which means money for local businesses. We all benefit."

"I know, I know," Will conceded. "I'm happy to help."

"Community engagement," Roman added. "And the kids love it when we let them sit in the truck. Anyway, thought I'd give you a heads-up. Meeting at six, Town Hall."

"I'll be there," Will promised, ending the call.

##

Will parked his ute on the street outside the SES headquarters just after sunset and made his way inside, nodding greetings to familiar faces. He spotted Roman chatting with Nancy Westbury from the IGA store and made his way over to them.

"Will! Right on time," Roman clapped him on the shoulder. The SES captain was a solid man with black hair flecked with silver, his powerful build testament to decades of physical work. "You know Nancy?"

"Course I do," Will smiled at the older woman. Nancy still had the grey permed hair she'd had when he was a kid buying lollies at the store after school.

"Hello, Will. How are you?"

He wondered how long it would be before the sympathy left everyone's tone when they greeted him.

"I'm very well, thank you, Nancy. Busy as usual. You?"

"Business is good." Her eyes twinkled. "Not such a big call for lollies since you grew up, though, Will."

Will chuckled and headed over to the chairs.

"Alright, people, let's get started," Roman called, moving to the front of the room. The chatter died down as everyone found seats. Will sat next to Jon Kendall, who had just arrived and sat in a row of vacant chairs.

"Where's Joe?" Will asked, looking around for the third member of their usual trio.

"Running late," Jon replied. "Said something about dropping Violet off at the Fig Tree Lodge. Another committee meeting, I think. But I could be wrong. It's hard to keep up with those women."

Will nodded, turning his attention to Roman as the meeting began.

"Alrighty. First thing on the agenda today." He looked up from his notes and grinned. "I'm sure you've all heard about Edwina Lette's latest ambitious plan?"

A collective groan, only half-joking, rose from the assembled volunteers. "You mean her Christmas in July thing. Isn't one Christmas enough? Do we have to have it twice this year?" someone called from the back row, and there were chuckles around the room.

"The parade will be on Saturday, the nineteenth of July, moving from Fred's Garage along Main Street to the Showground," Roman said, consulting his notes. "The committee would like both the RFS and SES to participate again. Last year's fire truck with the fairy lights was a big hit with the kids." There were nods around the room. "So, everyone's happy to be in?" Roman looked around at his team. There were no objections. "Okay, we're in. Same as last year—fire truck, lights, volunteers in uniform. Maybe we'll add a Santa hat to the truck this time."

As the discussion moved on, Will managed to avoid volunteering for the float, but he would tell Roman later that he was happy to help behind the scenes. The rest of the meeting focused on the winter firewood scavenging and clean-up scheduled for the end of the month. Teams were assigned to different areas, with Will volunteering to oversee the clean-up in the eastern section of the shire, bordering his own property.

As the meeting drew to a close, Nancy raised her hand. "May I speak?"

"Of course," Roman said with a smile.

"A new music teacher is starting at the high school next week. She'll be directing the Christmas play and organising carols for the festival. Jaclyn Rossiter asked me to see if any of our SES members have musical talents you've been hiding. Now's the time to volunteer."

Will was suddenly aware of Jon nudging him in the ribs. He shot his friend a questioning look.

"Didn't you used to sing in that band at ag college?" Jon whispered, a mischievous glint in his eye.

"That was fifteen years ago," Will muttered back, "and it was two gigs at the campus pub, not exactly a musical career."

But Jon had already raised his hand. "Will here has a decent voice, Nancy. And I know he can play the piano. Might be able to help out."

Will's cheeks heated as several heads turned towards him, including Roman's.

"Is that so, Will?" he asked, looking pleased. "That would be wonderful. The new teacher—Beth Curtis is her name—could probably use some adult volunteers. Most of the high school boys are too cool to participate, you know how it is."

"I really don't think—" Will began, but Roman cut him off.

"Good man, Will. Community spirit!"

Will shot Jon a look that promised retribution, but his mate merely grinned back, unrepentant.

The meeting wrapped up shortly after, with final assignments for the winter clean-up distributed and dates confirmed. As they walked out together, Jon clapped Will on the shoulder.

"Before you murder me for volunteering you," he said, "let me make it up to you. Cleo's invited the new teacher for a barbeque next Sunday. Jaclyn and Ryan, and Violet and Jo will be there too, plus Mark and Leah. Why don't you join us?"

"It would be great to catch up with everyone. I'm keen to hear what Mark is doing with the vineyard." Will frowned. "But if this is another one of your matchmaking attempts—"

"It's a barbie with friends," Jon insisted, though the innocent expression didn't quite reach his eyes. "Nothing more. Cleo just wants to make sure Beth feels welcome, and you know how Cleo is—the more the merrier."

Will hesitated. He was curious about the newcomer, but he also knew his friends well enough to recognise a setup when he saw one. Still, a dinner at the Kendalls' place was hardly a life commitment, and it would be good to meet the new teacher.

"Fine," he conceded. "But no obvious matchmaking, alright? The poor woman's probably been overwhelmed enough without you two playing Cupid."

"Scout's honour," Jon promised, raising his hand in a mock salute. "Just a friendly get-together. Sunday, four o'clock."

As Will drove home, he wondered about the new music teacher from Sydney. He knew that Jaclyn Rossiter had had trouble finding a music teacher when the school expanded last year. Most of the new staff had been teachers from rural areas. He wondered what would bring a city woman to a small town like Bindarra Creek? And why was he even thinking about it?

Bindarra Creek was a small town, and newcomers were a source of interest and conversation, he told himself. Nothing more than that because he was too busy to harbour any secret hope that Beth Curtis might be someone who could appreciate the quiet beauty of country life.

Will pushed the thought away as he turned into his driveway. He had more important things to worry about than a woman he hadn't even met yet. There were ewes to check in the morning, fencing to finish, and a farm that demanded his full attention.

Still, as Will moved around his silent kitchen, heating a tin of tomato soup, he hummed under his breath. It had been a long time since music had been part of his life.

Chapter Three

Beth stood outside the Cyprus Café, gathering her courage. It was ten minutes before seven on Monday evening, and the café was lit up warmly against the darkening sky. Through the windows, she could see several women already gathered around the large table at the back, chatting animatedly.

The Country Women's Association meeting. Her first real introduction to the Bindarra Creek community, beyond her initial days at the school. Beth's instinct was to turn around, go home, and come up with a plausible excuse for Jaclyn Rossiter in the morning. A migraine, perhaps. Or a burst pipe at the cottage.

But that would only delay the inevitable. Sooner or later, she would have to face these women, all of whom seemed to know more about her than she knew about them.

And she had to prepare for the barbeque next weekend at the Kendalls' farm.

Her first day at Bindarra Creek High School had gone reasonably well. Jaclyn Rossiter was lovely, and her philosophy for the school—focusing on the creative subjects—was close to Beth's heart. The students had been curious but respectful—most of them, anyway—and her colleagues had been welcoming, if a bit too interested in her background. She'd managed to deflect most of the personal questions, focusing instead on her plans for the music program. Beth was satisfied with the first week; despite the unexpected Christmas play responsibility, which was a given apparently, she was pretty sure she'd made the right decision in coming to Bindarra Creek.

Taking a deep breath, she pushed open the café door. The bell jangled, and several heads turned toward her.

"Beth! You made it!" Claire called from behind the counter, where she was arranging a platter of biscuits. "Come in, come in. We're just getting started."

Beth summoned a smile and moved toward the group of women. There were about a dozen of them, ranging in age from around thirty to well into their seventies. She recognised Edwina and Thea from the day she'd arrived in town, and Jaclyn and Cleo were there from the school.

Claire gestured for her toward an empty chair. "Everyone, this is Beth Curtis, our new music teacher. Beth, this is... well, most of the CWA committee. You know Jaclyn and Cleo, of course …" She ran through all the names, and Beth tried to remember them.

Claire continued with introductions, but the names and faces began to blur together. Beth smiled and nodded, trying to commit at least a few details to memory.

"We're so pleased you could join us," Edwina said. She was an older woman with waist-length grey hair. "We've been without proper musical direction for the Christmas play for too long."

"I'm happy to help," Beth replied automatically, though 'happy' was far from what she was feeling. "Though I should warn you, I'm still finding my way at the school."

"Oh, don't worry about that," Thea said with a dismissive wave. She was a plump, energetic woman with dark curly hair and a Greek accent. "The play is very simple. We do it every year, just change it a little. The children know the songs already."

This was news to Beth. "Oh? What exactly is the play?"

"We usually do a modified version of 'A Christmas Carol', at presentation day at the end of the school year," Cleo explained. "But with Australian elements. The ghost of Christmas Past shows Scrooge an Australian colonial Christmas, Christmas Present is a modern Aussie beach Christmas, that sort of thing."

Jaclyn intervened. "Perhaps it's time for a fresh story?"

"That's a great idea," Cleo said. "The songs were a bit old-fashioned. The kids hated them, and the community has seen the play several times."

"What do you think, Beth?" Edwina held her gaze with bright hazel eyes.

"I'm sure I can come up with something. How long have I got?" Beth felt a small measure of relief. At least she wouldn't be compared with previous productions.

"Three months until performance night."

Claire placed a large pot of tea and the plate of biscuits on the table, then took a seat beside Beth. "Let's get started, shall we? The festival's only a few months away, and there's a lot to coordinate."

Sue nodded and pulled out a folder. "First item on the agenda—the overall schedule. We've got the cooking classes starting in May, running through to July. Thea, you're handling the Greek cuisine class?"

"Yes, and Maria Fukuka is doing Japanese and Vito, Italian."

Beth listened as the women discussed the cooking class schedule, making notes in a small book she'd brought along. It seemed that the Christmas in July festival was far more elaborate than she'd realised, with events spanning several months and culminating in the July parade and play.

"Now, for the parade," Claire continued, turning to a new page in her folder. "The various community groups have committed to the floats. The Lette family is doing their historical float again, the RFS and SES are participating, the school will have a float..."

"And we need the students to perform carols during the parade," Edwina added, looking directly at Beth. "A small choir, perhaps? They could perform at various stops along the route."

Beth felt all eyes on her. "I... I'd need to see

how many students are interested. And we'd need to rehearse... and probably need to organise some instruments." The last thing Beth was going to commit to was being a part of the performance. "Perhaps we have some local musicians who could assist?"

"Of course, dear," Edwina said soothingly. "No one expects perfection. It's just about creating a festive atmosphere."

Cleo jumped up. "I've got a great idea. Will Greaves plays the piano. Could we get one up on the float?"

"I'm sure with all those muscled men in the RFS and the SES, they could get one on a truck," Thea suggested.

Edwina chuckled. "Since when have you been looking at muscled men, Thea Levonis?"

Laughter ran around the room, and Thea beamed as she leaned over to Beth. "They are teasing me," she said. "My Stavros is a wonderful husband."

The meeting continued, with responsibilities assigned and timelines established. Beth found herself agreeing to direct the Christmas play with performances scheduled for the last weekend of July, organise a student choir for the parade, and coordinate with various community groups who wanted to incorporate music into their parade floats. The scope was overwhelming—cooking classes running from May through July, starting with preserves and jams in early May, followed by gingerbread houses the next day. There would be movie screenings at the old cinema, starting with a special Friday night opening of *Love Actually*, carol singers performing throughout July, and even a drone light show finale on the last day of July in Lette Park.

"There's also Meg and Jack's wedding on July twelfth," Claire added with a smile. "At Mary Moonie's Museum, with the reception at the Riverside Pub. It should be a beautiful, clear day for it. And Dan's organising a karaoke night on the eighteenth—Christmas songs only—with a romantic getaway as the prize at one of Stevie Ryan's Stars Cottages."

"It's a big weekend, with the Carols by Candlelight on the twentieth in Lette Park," Cleo chimed in. "And Edwina's planning a fortune-telling tent for several events. Though we'll need to hope for clearer skies than this," she added, glancing toward the rain-streaked windows.

Beth glanced around the room at the enthusiastic women, unable to believe what was being planned.

And here I was thinking I was coming to a quiet country town. Even the large suburban school in Sydney hadn't been involved in such a big community event.

By the time the formal meeting ended and the conversation shifted to more general town gossip, Beth was feeling slightly overwhelmed. She sipped her tea, trying to process everything she'd just committed to.

"It's a lot to take in, isn't it?" Claire said quietly, noticing Beth was quiet.

"A bit," Beth admitted. "I wasn't expecting to be quite so involved."

Claire patted her hand sympathetically. "The first year in town is always the most challenging. But you won't be doing it alone. We all pitch in." She glanced around the table. "That's the beauty of small-town life. Everyone helps everyone else."

Beth wasn't sure if that was reassuring or terrifying. In Sydney, she'd been accustomed to professional boundaries and clear delineations between work and personal life. Here, it seemed, those lines were far more blurred.

Not that that had done her much good. David had always been disparaging about her 'little school performances".

The conversation around the table had turned to the winter firewood clean-up scheduled for the weekend after next. Beth half-listened, gathering that it was some kind of community service event where volunteers cleared fallen timber from local properties.

"Beth, will you be joining the clean-up?" Violet had been a late arrival, and Beth hadn't noticed her sitting at the end until she spoke. "It's a wonderful way to meet people, and the high school always sends a contingent of students for community service credits."

"It's two weekends away, so it won't overlap with the barbeque at our place this Sunday," Cleo said.

"I hadn't heard about it until now," Beth confessed. "But if the school is involved, I suppose I should be too."

Jaclyn caught her eye and smiled, with an almost imperceptible nod.

"Wonderful!" Claire beamed. "It starts at

eight. Wear sturdy clothes and boots. The SES organises everything—they'll have gloves and tools."

Beth was about to ask for more details when the café door opened, letting in a blast of cold air. She turned to see a tall man entering, carrying a stack of firewood. He was broad-shouldered, with light brown hair that curled slightly at the collar of his flannel shirt, and the lean, muscled build of someone who worked outdoors.

"Evening, ladies," he called, moving toward the counter. "Sorry to interrupt, but I've brought the firewood Nico asked me to drop in."

"Perfect timing, Will!" Claire exclaimed, standing. "We've just finished the formal part of the meeting. Put it by the wood stove, would you?"

Will nodded, making his way past the table. His eyes swept over the group, pausing briefly on Beth before continuing to the wood stove in the corner.

"Will Greaves," Claire explained quietly to Beth, "has a sheep station out on Avon Road. Best merino wool in the district. Also volunteers with the SES. He's the piano player."

Will returned from stacking the wood, wiping his hands on his jeans. Claire waved him over. "Will, this is Beth Curtis, our new music teacher. Beth, Will Greaves."

Will extended his hand, and Beth shook it, noticing the calluses and strength in his grip. "Welcome to Bindarra Creek," he said, his voice deep and pleasant. "How are you settling in?"

"Slowly getting there," Beth admitted. "But everyone's been very welcoming."

"Good to hear." His smile was warm but brief, his eyes a clear blue-grey that reminded Beth of the winter sky. "Cleo mentioned you might come to the clean-up at the end of the month?"

"Apparently so," Beth said, glancing at Cleo. "Though I'm not entirely sure what's involved."

"It's straightforward enough," Will explained. "We clear fallen timber from properties, reduce fire hazards, and distribute the wood to those who need it for heating. There will be high school students who come along and they usually help with the lighter work—gathering smaller branches, sorting wood, that kind of thing."

"That sounds... very physical," Beth commented, trying to imagine herself and her students engaged in manual labour.

A smile tugged at the corner of Will's mouth. "It is. But it's good work and important for the community. We provide all the equipment and training. No one's expected to do more than they're comfortable with."

"I'll be there," she found herself saying. "With whatever students volunteer."

"Great," Will nodded. "We meet at the SES shed headquarters. We'll assign teams and areas there." He lifted his hand in a wave. "Bye, ladies. I should get going. Early start tomorrow."

"Thank you for the wood, Will," Thea said. "Nico will sort the payment."

Will nodded again, said a general goodbye to the group, and headed for the door. As he left, Beth noticed several of the women watching him with speculative expressions.

"Now there's a man who knows the meaning of hard work," Edwina commented, not particularly quietly. "Been running that farm single-handed since his grandfather and his parents died within a year of each other. And he still finds time to volunteer with the SES."

"And he's not bad to look at, either," Thea added with a wink towards Beth, who felt herself colouring slightly.

"Ladies, please," Claire interjected, though she was smiling too. "Let's not embarrass our new teacher. Will Greaves is a pillar of the community; that's all Beth needs to know for now."

"And single," Thea murmured just loud enough for Beth's ears.

The conversation moved on, but Beth found herself thinking about Will. He had been less inquisitive and more interested in matters at hand than quizzing her. His manner hadn't caused her to feel as tense as she had been. Will Greaves hadn't seemed interested in her, or maybe she was getting used to meeting new people.

When the meeting closed, Beth noticed she'd filled several pages of her notebook with notes and tasks. The Christmas play alone would require auditions, rehearsals, costume coordination, and music arrangement, not to mention finding a suitable play to perform and the musical arrangement. And that was just one element of the festival.

"Feeling overwhelmed?" Cleo asked, appearing at Beth's side as she put on her coat.

Beth managed a smile. "Am I that obvious?"

"First-timer at a CWA meeting? It's normal," Cleo assured her. "But you know what helps?"

"What?"

"Friends," Cleo said simply. "Which is why you're coming to the barbeque at our place on Sunday," she added as Beth began to protest. "No excuses. It'll be casual, just a few people. You've met most of them already."

Beth hesitated. She'd been planning to spend her evenings organising her classroom and preparing for the onslaught of festival responsibilities. But perhaps Cleo was right— maybe what she needed most was to feel less alone in her new community.

"Alright," she agreed. "That would be nice. Thank you."

Cleo beamed. "Perfect! Four o'clock. I'll show you where we live later."

Outside the café, the night air was cold and clear, stars pricking the black canopy of sky in a way very different from Sydney's light-polluted darkness. Beth pulled her coat closer around her as she walked to her car, her breath fogging in the autumn chill.

As she drove back to her cottage, she thought about what she'd committed to. It was daunting, particularly the Christmas play. The thought of standing in front of an audience, even directing rather than performing, made her stomach twist with anxiety.

David's voice echoed in her memory: *You're too rigid when you perform, Beth. Too technical. Where's the emotion? Where's the passion? This isn't a mathematical equation; it's music.*

She pushed the memory away, focusing on the road ahead. That was the past. This was a new beginning, a chance to rebuild her confidence and her career. If directing a small-town Christmas play and organising carol singers was part of that journey, then so be it.

As Beth walked up the front stairs of the small cottage she'd fallen in love with already, she reminded herself she wouldn't be doing it alone. Claire and the other women had made that clear. And soon, she'd have her first social occasion here and then the following weekend, a real introduction to community life in Bindarra Creek, working alongside Will Greaves and the other volunteers at the winter clean-up.

And she'd expected small-town life to be quiet!

Chapter Four

The rest of the week passed in a blur of classes and several interactions with the residents of Bindarra Creek. Beth's students, once they'd gotten over their initial curiosity about their new teacher from Sydney, proved to be enthusiastic and generally well-behaved. Several expressed interest in participating in the Christmas play, which was at least one worry partially addressed.

On Sunday afternoon, Beth drove out to the Kendalls' sheep farm and stood at the front door holding a bottle of wine, second-guessing her decision to accept Cleo's invitation to the barbeque. The casual gathering was meant to help her meet more of the community, but Beth's instinct was still to maintain her distance, despite the best efforts of the community to erode it.

"You came!" Cleo called from the front door, her face lighting up with pleasure. "Come through to the back—Jon's got the barbie going, and everyone's just arriving."

Beth followed Cleo through the house, admiring the comfortable family home with its mix of well-loved furniture and children's artwork adorning the walls. The back garden was spacious, with an established jacaranda tree providing shade over a large outdoor table, and Jon Kendall tending to a serious-looking barbecue setup.

"Beth!" Jon called, raising a beer in greeting. He was a solidly built man in his thirties with an easy smile and the relaxed manner of someone happy in his own skin. "Welcome to our humble weekend chaos. Hope you like lamb?"

"I do." Beth smiled, already feeling some of her tension ease. "Thank you for including me."

"Wouldn't hear of leaving you to spend Sunday alone," Cleo said firmly. "Now, let me introduce you to everyone. Jaclyn and Ryan are here somewhere—ah, there they are over near the herb garden."

"Beth!" Jaclyn came over with a warm smile, followed by the broad-shouldered man. "I'm so glad you could make it. This is my husband, Ryan—if you need anything fixed on your rental, he'll come and help you out."

"Lovely to meet you," Ryan said, extending his hand. "Jaclyn's been singing your praises all week. The students are very excited about having a proper music teacher again."

"They're great to work with," Beth replied. "Very enthusiastic, though I suspect some of that will wear off once the hard work of learning parts for the Christmas play begins."

"Speaking of which," Jac's eyes lit up, "how are you finding the festival preparations? Not too overwhelming, I hope? You can say no, you know."

Before Beth could answer, she heard a familiar voice calling her name. Violet appeared from around the side of the house, her copper hair catching the afternoon light, followed by a good-looking man who looked very much like Ryan.

"Beth! I was hoping you'd be here," Violet said, giving her a quick hug. "This is Joe—I've told him all about you. You've already met Ryan. He's Joe's big brother."

Joe offered a firm handshake and a broad smile. "Nice to meet you, Beth. Vi says you're settling in well, despite being thrown in the deep end with all the festival stuff."

"Some days better than others," Beth admitted with a laugh. "Though everyone's been very welcoming."

"That's the Bindarra way."

Beth turned to answer. An attractive woman with a wide smile and a tall man with short-cropped blond hair stood beside Violet.

"Mark and Leah." Cleo made the introductions. "These clever guys are developing a vineyard just out of town."

"Plus, I'm the part-time organiser for anything involving decorations. Edwina roped me in." Leah added with a self-deprecating smile. "I heard you're taking on the Christmas play—you're braver than I am."

"Or more foolish," Beth replied. "Though I'm hoping it's the former."

The conversation was interrupted by the sound of a vehicle pulling into the driveway. Will climbed out holding what appeared to be a covered dish and looking slightly formal in clean jeans and a button-down shirt.

"Will!" Jon called from the barbecue. "Perfect timing—I've just put the lamb on. Hope you brought your famous potato salad."

"As requested," Will replied, holding up the

dish. His eyes found Beth's across the garden, and he nodded a greeting that seemed both pleased and slightly uncertain.

"You remember Will, Beth?" Cleo asked with studied casualness that didn't fool anyone. "From the CWA meeting?"

"We've met," Beth confirmed, feeling heat rise in her cheeks as several pairs of interested eyes moved between them. "Will, Jaclyn said you've offered to help with set construction for the play. Thank you."

"Practical help," Will added quickly, moving to place his dish on the outdoor table. "Nothing too creative."

"Don't let him fool you," Jaclyn interjected. "Will's got quite the artistic streak. You should see the garden sculptures he makes from old farm equipment. They're wonderful."

Will shrugged, and his cheeks coloured. "Just something to do when it's raining. Not that we've had much of that lately."

Beth found herself curious about this artistic side of him, but before she could ask, Jon announced that the first round of meat was ready, and everyone gravitated toward the barbeque area where a large table was set.

Conversation flowed around the large table, interspersed with lots of laughter. Excited chatter from the children playing on the swings added to the happy gathering, and Beth found herself relaxing in a way she hadn't done for a long time.

"How are you finding the transition from Sydney?" She looked up; Will had moved to the seat beside her. Ryan had gone to deal with a crying child.

Beth considered her answer carefully. "Different, certainly. The pace is slower, but in some ways there's more... intensity. Everything seemed to be quite public."

Will nodded but didn't speak.

"That can be challenging," Leah agreed sympathetically. "When I first moved here, I felt like I was living in a fishbowl. But there are benefits too."

"Like having half the town turn out when our roof leaked during that storm last winter," Mark added with a grin. "I've never seen so many people with buckets and tarps appear so quickly."

"Community spirit," Will said quietly. "It's a town where you know you can rely on help when you need it."

"Beth, have you given any more thought to the adult choir idea?" Jaclyn asked. "Several people have asked about it since word got around about your background."

That usual flutter of anxiety hit. "I'm not sure I'll have time to manage both a student production and an adult choir. Not yet, anyway. The Christmas play alone is going to be quite demanding. And I've already taken on a piano student. Meg McGregor."

"What if it was just carol singing?" Violet suggested. "Nothing too formal—just a group to perform during the parade and maybe at the Carols by Candlelight evening?"

"You could always recruit some helpers," Cleo added with a meaningful glance toward Will. "Share the load."

Will caught the look and shook his head with amusement. "I think Beth already knows my talents run more to carpentry than conducting."

"Everyone has musical ability," Beth found herself saying, then paused, surprised by her own words. "I mean, it's more about willingness to participate than natural talent."

"See?" Cleo said triumphantly. "You're a natural teacher. You'll have the whole town singing in harmony before you know it."

The conversation flowed, but Beth became aware of Will watching her. His expression relaxed her even more.

She retreated slightly, not sure how to deal with the warmth that had settled in her chest.

Be careful. Remember how David made me think he was something he wasn't.

As darkness closed in, everyone started packing up, and those with children rounded them up. Beth helped Cleo clear the table, grateful for the chance to express her thanks privately.

"This was lovely," she said as they stacked plates in the kitchen. "Thank you for including me."

"Thank you for coming," Cleo replied warmly. "I know it can't be easy starting over in a new place. But you're fitting in beautifully."

"I'll see you at school tomorrow. Thank Jon for me, too."

Outside, Beth found Will standing beside his ute, the other guests having already departed with waves and promises to catch up soon.

"That potato salad was the best I've ever eaten," Beth said.

"Thank you, it was my mum's recipe. Did you have a good afternoon?" he asked as she approached.

"Very good," Beth admitted. "Your friends are lovely."

"They're good people," Will agreed. "How's school? What you expected?"

Beth put her head to the side. "Overwhelming sometimes. In Sydney, I could teach my classes and go home for the weekend, and then not see anyone until the next week. Here, everything seems to overlap."

"That can be challenging," Will acknowledged. "But there are benefits too. When someone needs help, the whole town turns out."

"Like the winter clean-up?"

"Exactly like that." Will smiled. "It started as a practical response to fire hazards, but it's grown over the years."

They stood in comfortable silence for a moment, looking at the brilliant sky.

"About the Christmas play," Will said finally. "If you *do* need help with the practical aspects—set construction, moving equipment, that sort of thing—I am happy to help."

"That would be... very helpful. Thank you."

"Just let me know what you need," Will said simply. He hesitated, then added, "And Beth? Don't let them pressure you into anything you're not comfortable with. The carol singing, performing—let it be your choice."

The perceptive comment caught Beth off guard. How had he picked up on her anxiety about performing when she'd tried so hard to hide it?

"Thank you," she said softly. "That means more than you might realise."

"We don't want you burning out." Will nodded, then climbed into his ute. "See you at the clean-up next Saturday?"

"I'll be there," Beth confirmed. "With however many students I can convince to get up early on a weekend."

As Will drove away with a wave, Beth stood watching the ute disappear down the road.

She smiled. Perhaps this community thing wouldn't be so hard after all.

Chapter Five

Saturday dawned cold and clear, with frost glittering on the grass outside Beth's cottage window. She dressed in layers—old jeans, a warm sweater, and the sturdiest boots she owned—feeling slightly ridiculous but determined to honour her commitment to the SES winter clean-up. The prospect of manual labour still concerned her, but Will's reassuring words at the CWA meeting stayed with her: 'There are jobs for all skill levels.'

At seven-thirty, Beth loaded her small group of volunteer students into the school minibus and headed for the SES headquarters. The morning air was crisp and invigorating, though she noticed several of the teenagers looking distinctly unenthusiastic about their early start.

"Come on, you lot," she said with forced cheerfulness. "Think of it as character building."

"Miss, why couldn't we do character building at a more reasonable hour?" groaned Eddie Taylor, one of her more vocal students.

"Because trees don't fall down at convenient times," Beth replied, surprising herself with how naturally the country logic came to her.

The SES shed was already bustling with activity when they arrived. Volunteers of all ages milled about, checking equipment and receiving instructions from Roman Taylor. Beth spotted several familiar faces from the CWA meeting, including Claire McGregor.

"Beth!" Will appeared at her elbow, looking entirely at home in work clothes and heavy boots. "Good to see you. And you brought reinforcements."

"Ten eager volunteers," Beth said, gesturing to her students who were eyeing the collection of chainsaws, axes, and safety equipment with varying degrees of interest and alarm.

"Don't worry," Will grinned. "We'll start them on the sorting and stacking. Nothing too dangerous."

Roman called for attention, and the assembled volunteers gathered around for the morning briefing. Properties had been assigned to different teams, with the eastern section— bordering Will's farm—designated for Beth's group under Will's supervision.

"Remember," Roman emphasised, "safety first. No one works alone with power tools, everyone wears the provided safety gear, and if you're not sure about something, ask. The goal is to clear fire hazards, not create hospital patients."

A nervous shiver ran down Beth's spine as they loaded into various vehicles and headed out to their assigned areas. The countryside looked different in the early morning light—more rugged than it appeared from the road.

Will's ute led their small convoy down a dirt track to a property where storm damage from the previous winter had left numerous fallen branches and several downed trees scattered across paddocks. The landowner, an elderly man named Frank Peterson, met them at the gate with obvious relief.

"Can't tell you how much I appreciate this," he said, shaking Will's hand. "Been worrying about fire season with all this dry timber lying about."

"That's what we're here for," Will replied easily. "We'll have this cleaned up in no time."

The next few hours passed in a blur of organised activity. Will proved to be an excellent teacher, patiently showing Beth and the students how to safely move and stack timber, which pieces were suitable for firewood, and which needed to go into the burn pile. The work was harder than Beth had expected, but there was something satisfying about the physical effort and the visible results as the paddock slowly cleared.

"You're a natural at this," Will commented during a brief break, watching Beth efficiently sort a pile of branches. "Sure you've never done farm work before?"

"Positive," Beth laughed, pulling off her work gloves to survey her already blistered hands. "Though I'm beginning to understand why you brought that thermos of strong coffee this morning."

"Strong coffee's as vital as good boots." His expression was serious, but as their eyes met, his face split into a wide grin that Beth found it hard to look away from.

By midday, the transformation of the property was remarkable. What had been a chaotic scatter of fallen timber was now organised into neat piles—firewood stacked and ready for collection by those who needed it, burn material safely contained, and the paddock cleared and safe.

"Time for lunch," Roman announced as the various teams regrouped at the SES shed. A barbeque had been set up in the adjacent park, with volunteers bringing salads and sides to share.

Beth sat at a picnic table with Will, several of her students, and a mix of RFS and SES volunteers.

"Not too sore?" Will asked quietly, noticing Beth favouring her right shoulder.

"Nothing that won't heal," she assured him. "Though I suspect I'll feel it more tomorrow."

"First time's always the hardest," Claire observed from across the table. "But you did well, Beth. Some of the townies who've joined us barely last an hour before making excuses to leave."

"My students were the real heroes," Beth deflected. "They worked harder than I expected."

"Because you were working alongside them," Will pointed out. "Leadership by example. They respect that."

The simple observation pleased Beth more

than it probably should have. In Sydney, respect from students felt like something she constantly had to earn and re-earn in the classroom and the playground. Here, it seemed to flow more naturally from shared effort and mutual consideration. She didn't feel like a teacher when she was out there working with them.

As the afternoon wound down and volunteers began departing, Beth helped load the remaining equipment into the SES vehicles. Her muscles ached, her hands were blistered, and she suspected she'd be finding sawdust in her hair and clothes for days. But there was also a deep satisfaction she hadn't experienced in years.

"Thank you," she said to Will as they walked back to their vehicles. "For including me, for being patient with my complete inexperience, and for making me feel useful."

"Thank you for coming," Will replied. "And for bringing the students. It made a difference, having those ten extra pairs of hands."

They reached the minibus, where her tired students were already piling in, chattering about the day's work.

"Will there be more of these?" Beth found

herself asking. "Other community work days, I mean."

"Always something," Will confirmed. "Especially coming up to fire season. And then there's the float preparation—plenty of opportunities for community involvement if you're interested."

"I think I am," Beth admitted, surprising herself. "Interested, I mean."

Will's smile was warm. "I'm glad. Bindarra Creek needs interested people."

That warmth when Will was around settled a little bit deeper.

***

Will guided his ute carefully along the rutted track that led to the eastern boundary of his property, going over the tasks that would need attention after the weekend. The fencing in the lower paddock needed repair, the shearing shed required cleaning and preparation for the upcoming season, and he'd noticed one of the ewes showing early signs of lambing, weeks ahead of schedule.

But despite the pressing workload of his farm, Will couldn't stop thinking about Beth Curtis. Not only was she one of the prettiest women he'd ever met, with her dark curly hair, fair skin, and rosy cheeks, but she also had the sweetest smile he'd managed to coax out of her a few times today. He wondered what had happened to her to make her so reticent.

The memory of that smile made something tighten in his chest—an unfamiliar feeling. There had been something about the way she'd looked at him when she thought he wasn't watching. It stirred a protective instinct in him that went beyond simple attraction. He wanted to know what put those shadows in her eyes, what made her flinch when someone moved too close to her, and what had taught her to keep her guard up even in moments of laughter.

Will pulled the ute to a stop near the damaged fence line but made no move to get out. Instead, he sat there, hands still gripping the steering wheel, thinking about the careful way Beth had spoken to him. He'd seen that kind of wariness before, in animals that had been mistreated, and it made his jaw clench with anger at whoever had hurt her.

The strangest part was how natural it had felt to be near her, despite that. When she'd accidentally brushed his hand while reaching for the thermos of coffee, the brief contact had sent warmth shooting up his arm. And when she'd finally relaxed enough to laugh at something Eddie Taylor had said, the sound had been like music—rusty from disuse, but lovely.

He couldn't remember a time when a woman had occupied his thoughts this way. The demands of running the farm alone had left little room for romance or relationships after Melissa, and he was content with his solitary life. But Beth had stirred something in him that he'd thought was buried for good. The way she'd looked in the afternoon light, sitting on the veranda with the other women, had made him forget about everything else.

He sat there, planning excuses to visit town again before the weekend. Maybe the hardware store needed his business, or perhaps he could turn up at the school to see when Beth wanted him to help with the set construction. Maybe that would be an excuse to get her number. Anything to see her again, to maybe earn another one of those rare, precious smiles that seemed to light her up from within.

He shook his head. This fence wouldn't repair itself, and Beth Curtis—whatever her story—probably had enough troubles without a lovesick farmer adding to them.

Chapter Six

Beth surveyed the school hall, considering the furniture and decorations needed to create the Victorian parlour scene that would be central to the Christmas play. In the end, the students had voted on a version of the usual play with a revamped script. Beth had worked with Jenny Lyons, the English teacher, and the students were rewriting the script under Jenny's supervision. It had developed surprisingly well with a gentle touch of humour.

The auditions last Monday had gone well, with a talented group of students eager to participate. Billy Kendall-Cummings, Jon and Cleo's nephew, a charismatic senior with a surprisingly rich baritone, had been the obvious choice for Scrooge, while Kaylee Miller, a Year Ten student with ballet training, would play the Ghost of Christmas Past.

What Beth hadn't expected was Will Greaves, appearing in the doorway looking slightly out of place in jeans and a clean flannel shirt, his hair still damp as though he'd just showered after a day's work.

"We didn't get a chance to discuss the play sets last weekend," Will said as Beth walked across the hall, her heels clicking on the timber floor. "I've been meaning to come in before this, but I had a farm emergency."

"I hope all's well now."

Will nodded, and the aroma of fresh soap wafted over as she stood beside him. "It is. But I'm still available to help with the sets if I'm not too late."

"That's great," Beth said. "The script calls for three main scenes—the Victorian parlour for Scrooge's home, a colonial Australian Christmas for the Past section, and a modern beach Christmas for the Present section. Nothing too elaborate, but definitely beyond my carpentry skills, which are non-existent."

Will nodded thoughtfully. "Sounds manageable. When do you need them ready?"

"We start rehearsals with the full cast next week, but we can work with taped outlines on the floor initially. The sets would need to be completed by early July for dress rehearsals."

"I can work with that timeline," Will confirmed. "I'll need measurements of the stage area, and maybe some rough sketches of what you're envisioning."

"I can provide those," Beth said, feeling a weight lift from her shoulders. One more aspect of the daunting Christmas play that she wouldn't have to handle alone.

"I saw the light on as I drove past," Will said. "You're at school late."

"Time got away. The cleaner just asked me if I was about to go so she can set the alarms."

"Could I walk you to your car?" he asked. "It's dark outside now."

Beth hesitated only briefly. "Thank you, that would be nice."

Outside, the evening was cool but pleasant, stars beginning to appear in the clear sky. They walked in companionable silence for a moment, Beth's thoughts turning to the Christmas play and all the work ahead.

"You seemed more relaxed tonight," Will observed. "Was the responsibility of the play bothering you?"

The question was perceptive enough to bring a twinge of discomfort. "Partly," she admitted. "It's a lot of pressure, being new to town and immediately having to produce something the whole community will attend and judge."

Will nodded. "Everyone watching, everyone with an opinion."

"Exactly." Beth was grateful for his perception. "In Sydney, I could be anonymous outside of school. Here, I'm 'the new music teacher' everywhere I go."

They reached her car, and Beth turned to face Will, finding him studying her with a thoughtful expression.

"For what it's worth," he said quietly, "I think you'll do a wonderful job with the play. You care about doing it right, and that matters more than experience."

The simple vote of confidence touched Beth more deeply than she'd expected. "Thank you. That... means a lot."

Will nodded, seeming slightly embarrassed. "Well, I should let you get home." He hesitated. "Um, I came into town to grab some dinner at the Riverside pub. Do you have dinner plans? Maybe we could grab a pizza or something and work on these sets?"

Her heart skipped unexpectedly. It had been so long since anyone had asked her to dinner and looked at her with keen interest.

Her first instinct was to decline, to retreat to the solitude of her cottage. But standing there, seeing the kindness in Will's eyes, she changed her mind.

"I…" she began, then paused.

Am I making a big mistake? Did I learn nothing in Sydney?

"I'd like that," she said, and she meant it.

Her acceptance seemed to surprise them both. Will's face brightened with a pleased smile.

***

The Riverside pub was busier than usual for a weeknight, but Will was grateful for the familiar atmosphere. He watched Beth as they entered, noting how her face lit up when several people greeted her warmly. Claire McGregor from the CWA gave her a big smile, and a couple of parents from the school waved to her. Will could see Beth relaxing by degrees, her shoulders losing some of their tension as she realised she was genuinely welcomed here.

They found a quiet table near the window, and after consulting with Beth, Will ordered a Margherita pizza to share, along with drinks. The conversation started carefully with safe topics that wouldn't spook her. But gradually, as the wine loosened her tongue and the pub atmosphere worked its magic, Beth began to open up.

When she mentioned studying performance at the conservatorium, Will felt a jolt of recognition.

"Life took some unexpected turns," she said.

The careful way she spoke about choosing teaching for stability told him there was pain there, disappointment perhaps, or something worse.

"I can understand that," he said gently. "Sometimes the practical choice and what your heart tells you have to co-exist."

When she asked about his path to farming, Will found himself sharing something he rarely talked about. "I spent a few years studying music myself, before Dad's first heart attack brought me home."

The surprise on Beth's face was worth the slight embarrassment he felt at the admission. In a town where he was known primarily as a sheep farmer, his musical background felt like a secret identity.

"I was at ag college, and I took some private

lessons. Piano, mainly. Some guitar," he said. "I know it doesn't fit the image of a rugged sheep farmer." He lifted his arms and flexed his muscles.

Beth's delighted laugh sent a tingle along his nerve endings. "That's wonderful. Do you still play?"

"When I can. There's an old upright piano in the homestead that belonged to my grandmother. I'd always played by ear, but I decided to get those lessons when I was in Wagga. The piano has seen better days, but it still holds a tune." He grinned, feeling more relaxed. "Mostly, I play for the sheep. They're a very appreciative audience."

Beth laughed again, and her whole face lit up. "I must admit I already knew you played. It was suggested you could play Christmas carols on a piano from a float at the parade."

Will groaned, covering his face. The last thing he needed was to become the CWA's latest project. "Please tell me you didn't encourage that idea."

The mischievous smile that crossed Beth's face was worth every ounce of potential embarrassment. "I could have mentioned that musical accompaniment could add something special to the parade, but I refrained."

"Beth Curtis, you are a dangerous woman," he said, but he was grinning despite himself. There was something intoxicating about this playful side of her, so different from the careful, guarded woman of their first couple of meetings.

As they shared pizza and stories, Will loved every smile, every laugh. When Cathy Kendall-Cummings stopped at their table to tell her how excited Billy was about being in the play, Beth's cheeks were rosy with delight. For the first time, he noticed her cute dimple when she smiled.

She belongs here. She just needs time to see that for herself.

"You're settling in well," he said carefully when Cathy left. "I can see it in your face—you look more at home."

"I feel at home. And I'm more surprised every day. I've only been here two weeks!"

Will went to the counter to pay, and Beth followed. When she tried to pay half, he shook his head. "Next time," he said with a smile.

"Okay, next time," she said, and Will felt as

though he was walking on air as they walked out to the car park.

"I'll look forward to it," he said quietly.

"When can I hear you play?" she asked, smiling up at him as he stood beside her car.

"I guess I'll need to audition for you before you'll let me on that float."

"Absolutely." Her smile was warm. "I'll see you again soon."

Will stood there smiling until Beth's car was out of sight.

Chapter Seven

The next two weeks flew by, and Beth was more settled each day. The Christmas play rehearsals began in earnest, with Billy Kendall-Cummings proving to be a natural as Scrooge, bringing both humour and pathos to the role. Kaylee Miller was elegant and otherworldly as the Ghost of Christmas Past, while Gillian Fraser, a quiet but talented junior, surprised everyone with her powerful presence as the Ghost of Christmas Present.

Beth began to enjoy herself as the students' enthusiasm grew. The script, which had initially seemed simplistic, revealed unexpected charm and humour as the young actors brought it to life. The musical numbers, too, were coming together well, with several talented singers among the cast.

True to his word, Will had begun work on the set pieces, starting with the Victorian parlour that formed the central scene. He arrived at the school on weekday evenings after farm work, spending hours carefully constructing the framework of Scrooge's sitting room, complete with a functioning fireplace—electric, for safety—and period-appropriate furniture borrowed from various community members.

Beth often stayed late while he was there and worked on musical arrangements, and she found herself looking forward to Will's arrival each evening. They would exchange brief updates on their respective progress and talk about the other festival events.

One night, Beth was at the piano in the school hall, working through an arrangement of 'Good King Wenceslas' with an Australian twist. She was so absorbed in the music that she didn't hear Will enter, only becoming aware of his presence when she looked up to check a notation and saw him standing quietly near the stage.

"Sorry," he said when she startled slightly. "Didn't want to interrupt. That sounded great."

Beth felt that flush of embarrassment that always accompanied being overheard playing. "It's just a simple arrangement for the colonial Christmas scene. Nothing fancy."

Will approached the piano, curiosity evident

in his expression. "You changed the melody a bit. Made it sound more... I don't know, Australian somehow. How did you do that?"

Beth was surprised by his perception. "I modified the rhythm to reflect patterns you might hear in traditional indigenous music and shifted some of the harmonies to create a more open sound, like the landscape."

"It works," Will said simply. "Makes it recognisable but fresh."

His words warmed Beth unexpectedly. Unlike David's calculated praise designed to manipulate, or his cutting criticism meant to control, Will's observation was a simple appreciation of what he heard.

"Thank you," she said quietly. "It's still a work in progress."

Will nodded, then gestured towards the half-built set piece on the stage. "As is that. Would you mind if I keep working while you play? I find it easier to work with music."

"Not at all," Beth replied, though she felt a flutter of nerves at the thought of playing while being listened to. "I need to finalise this arrangement anyway."

She turned back to the piano, conscious of

Will moving to the stage and gathering his tools. For a moment, her fingers hovered uncertainly over the keys. Then she took a deep breath and began to play, forcing herself to focus on the music rather than her audience of one.

Gradually, the familiar rhythm took over, and Beth lost herself in the process of refining the arrangement. The sound of Will's measured sawing, careful hammering, and the occasional scrape of wood against wood became a counterpoint to her music, oddly complementary rather than intrusive.

After nearly an hour, Beth stretched her fingers and closed her sheet music. The arrangement was as complete as it could be for now, and fatigue was setting in after a long day of teaching and rehearsals.

"Finished?" Will asked, looking up from where he was securing a section of the fireplace mantel.

"For tonight," Beth confirmed, gathering her notes. "How's the set coming along?"

Will stood, wiping his hands on a cloth. "Making good progress. Should have the basic structure complete by next week, then it's just finer details and painting."

Beth approached the stage to look at what he'd done tonight. The fireplace was taking shape nicely, with a convincing mantelpiece and space for the electric flame unit that Edwina had sourced from a shed at her house.

"It's going to be perfect," she said, impressed. "I can't believe you're doing all this for us after full days on the farm."

Will shrugged, dismissing the praise. "It's a nice change of pace, actually. Different kind of work, using different skills."

"Still, I appreciate it. The students are so excited about having proper sets this year." Beth hesitated, then added, "Would you like a cup of tea? I was about to make one before heading home."

"I'd like that," Will said, setting down his tools. "Let me just clean up a bit first."

They moved to the small kitchenette adjacent to the hall, where Beth filled the electric kettle and pulled two mugs from the cupboard. The simple domesticity of the moment struck her—how comfortable it felt to be sharing this quiet task with Will after their respective work.

"How are the rehearsals going?" Will asked as they waited for the kettle to boil. "The students seem enthusiastic."

"They are," Beth confirmed, measuring tea leaves into a pot. "Billy is particularly good as Scrooge—he has a natural stage presence. And some of the younger students are surprisingly talented."

"Not surprising to you, though," Will observed. "You spotted their potential."

Beth smiled slightly. "That's the rewarding part of teaching—seeing students discover abilities they didn't know they had."

By the time they finished their tea and prepared to leave, Beth was reluctant to end the evening.

"How about I take you for pizza on Friday night to say thank you?" she ventured.

Will's smile was his answer.

As Beth drove home, she wondered if something more than friendship was developing between them. And if it was, could she trust it?

David's voice echoed in her memory: *You're too rigid, Beth. Too controlled. You'll never connect with an audience because you never truly connect with anything.*

She pushed the memory away firmly. David had been wrong about so many things. Perhaps he had been wrong about that, too. Perhaps her capacity for relationships wasn't the problem— perhaps it had been his inability to appreciate the depth of emotion beneath her controlled exterior.

Already, Will seemed to understand her and accept her as the person behind the music teacher.

Chapter Eight

Two weeks later, Will pulled up at the SES shed. Several vehicles were already parked outside, including Roman's distinctive dual-cab ute with the SES logo. He parked his ute and entered the building, greeted by the half a dozen members gathered around a large table covered in sketches and notes.

"There he is!" Roman called. "Our musical liaison. How's the piano playing coming along, Will?"

Will accepted the good-natured teasing with a slight smile. "First rehearsal is tomorrow evening. Beth—Miss Curtis—has selected the music."

"And you'll be singing too?" Jon asked, a mischievous gleam in his eye.

"Perhaps," Will replied, moving to examine the designs on the table. "What have we got here?"

"Float plans," Jon said. "It's taken a while. The RFS has picked a 'Christmas Under the Stars' theme for their float. We've had to put our thinking caps on."

"You're going to be busy," Jon commented as they walked to the Cyprus Café for a late lunch. "Farm, SES duties, play set construction, float building, and now carol singing. Not to mention your Friday night dates."

Friday pizza night with Beth had become a weekly event.

"I manage my time," Will replied. "And most of these commitments overlap anyway."

Jon's expression grew more serious. "Just be careful, mate. Beth seems nice, but from what Cleo's gathered, she's been through something rough in Sydney. And no one's sure if she's planning to stick around once the school year's over."

Will bristled slightly at the warning, though he knew it was because Jon was looking out for him. "I'm aware of that. We're friends, nothing more."

Jon raised his hands in mock surrender. "Fair enough. Just looking out for you. After Melissa—"

"This isn't like that," Will interrupted, more sharply than he intended. "Beth is nothing like Melissa."

"No, she's not," Jon agreed thoughtfully. "She seems more... considerate somehow." He shot Will a sidelong glance. "Which is why I think you like her so much."

Will couldn't entirely disagree with that assessment. Beth's lack of pretension, her commitment to her students, and her willingness to tackle community responsibilities despite her initial reservations—all these qualities appealed to him far more than Melissa's social ambitions ever had.

As they walked to the car, Jon glanced at his watch. "Fancy a quick beer at the Riverside? It's just past four."

Will considered the suggestion. The afternoon's farm chores could wait until tomorrow. "Why not?"

The Riverside Hotel sat on the banks of the Akuna River, its weathered timber facade and wide latticed verandas a testament to decades of serving the local community. Inside, the scent of hops and old timber greeted them, along with the low murmur of conversation from the handful of regulars scattered around the bar.

They ordered their beers and found a table near the window overlooking the river. The afternoon sun filtered through the gum trees, casting dappled shadows on the slow-moving water.

"So," Jon said, picking up his beer. "How's the farm going? You've seemed more settled lately."

Will rotated his glass thoughtfully. "Yeah, I finally feel as though I have my head around it. The irrigation's running smoothly, and I've got a handle on the crop rotation Dad always talked about but never properly explained."

"It's been a lot for you over the last four years," Jon said quietly.

Will nodded, remembering the overwhelming feeling he'd felt when the truck accident that had taken both his parents had thrust him into running the property. The sleepless nights, the constant worry about making the wrong decisions, the isolation of carrying it all alone.

Jon gave him a sideways glance as they finished their beers and headed for the utes. "It would be good if Beth did hang around."

Will held his eyes and grinned. "Yeah, it would."

Chapter Nine

When Will arrived at the high school on Tuesday evening, there were more people there than he and Beth. Students were helping to move the nearly completed set pieces into storage before the first carol rehearsal in the hall. The play sets had turned out well—the Victorian parlour with its fireplace and period furniture, the colonial veranda with roughly hewn benches and native flora, and the beach scene with its painted backdrop of ocean and sand.

Beth had been delighted with the results, particularly the attention to detail Will had incorporated—the carved mantelpiece in the parlour, the authentic-looking gum leaves and banksia for the colonial scene, the driftwood accents for the beach setting. The art students had added their talents with paint and decoration, bringing the sets to vibrant life.

"These look amazing," Beth said, surveying the completed pieces before they were carefully stored. "The students are so excited to be rehearsing with proper sets next week. I can't thank you enough."

"Happy to help," Will replied, pleased by her enthusiasm. "It's been an interesting project. Different from my usual work. I'll miss my nights here."

"Maybe you could join the choir for the carols?" Beth looked at him coyly before she ran her hand along the carved detail of the mantelpiece. "Have you ever thought about making furniture professionally? Or art pieces?"

Will shook his head. "It's just a hobby. Something to do in the evenings during the quiet seasons on the farm."

"Well, you're very good at it," Beth insisted. "Too good to keep it just as a hobby. Now, can I ask you to join my choir?"

The compliment warmed him, and Will had to refrain from puffing his chest out. He helped the student stagehands move the sets to the storage room, then returned to find the hall rearranged for the carol rehearsal, with chairs set in a semicircle around the piano. Eight parents had joined their students, and some of them were looking as nervous as he was. How could he say no when Beth had asked him so sweetly?

"How did you get roped in, mate?" Grant Cummings came to stand beside him.

Will shrugged. "Beth asked me to stay. What about you?"

"Cathy and Billy ganged up on me and said if I can sing in the shower every day, I can help out at the school." He looked rueful. "So here I am."

Beth stood at the piano, looking composed but with a subtle tension in her posture that Will had come to recognise as nervousness. She was still uncomfortable with public performance, though she concealed it well beneath professional confidence.

"Welcome, everyone," she began once all were seated. "Thank you for volunteering to join our students for the Christmas in July school choir. We'll be performing two items at the Carols by Candlelight."

As the rehearsal progressed, Beth transformed as her confidence kicked in. Her initial nervousness gave way to confident guidance, her musical expertise evident in how she helped each section refine their parts. This was Beth in her element—teaching and bringing out the best in each performer without drawing attention to herself.

They worked through several carols, with Beth providing piano accompaniment and occasional demonstrations of particularly challenging passages. Will was impressed by her voice—clear, pure, and expressively controlled. When she sang a brief solo to illustrate a phrasing technique, the room fell silent, captivated by the simple beauty of her singing.

"That's how the line should flow," she explained, seemingly unaware of the effect she'd had on her listeners. "Let's try it together now." Will joined in with gusto and enjoyed every moment.

By the end of the two-hour rehearsal, they had made impressive progress on two carols, with harmonies beginning to blend smoothly and the unique Australian elements becoming more pronounced. Beth dismissed them with thanks and a reminder of the next rehearsal date.

As the others began to disperse, Will lingered, helping to stack chairs and tidy the sheet music. Beth seemed lost in thought as she closed the piano and gathered her belongings. The students and parents quickly headed home for dinner.

"That went well," Will commented, approaching the piano. "The group sounds good together."

Beth looked up, her expression clearing. "It did, didn't it? Better than I expected for a first rehearsal. Everyone seems committed to making it work."

"Your arrangements are excellent," Will added. "The way you've adapted the traditional carols with Australian elements—It's clever without being gimmicky."

"Thank you," Beth said, a smile lighting her features. "I've been working on them for a couple of weeks."

'In your spare time?" he teased.

"It's nice to finally hear them sung rather than just imagined."

Will waited with her while she locked up and then walked beside her towards the parking lot, the evening cool but pleasant around them. Stars were appearing in the clear sky, and he looked up feeling very content.

"Would you like to see the stars properly?"

he asked before he could think. "From the farm, I mean. The view is incredible on clear nights like this—no town lights to interfere. Some of the best star-gazing in the region."

Beth looked taken aback by the invitation. "I'd like that," she said after a moment's hesitation. "I haven't done any star-gazing since coming to Bindarra."

"Friday, after our pizza?" Will suggested. "If it's clear, we could drive out to the eastern ridge. The view of the Milky Way from there is spectacular."

Beth nodded, a smile playing at the corners of her mouth. "Pizza and star-gazing. Sounds like a full evening."

"Too much?" Will asked, suddenly concerned he was pushing boundaries.

"No," Beth assured him quickly. "It sounds perfect. A nice break from play rehearsals and festival planning."

They reached their respective vehicles, pausing in the dimly lit parking lot. Will was acutely aware of Beth's proximity, of the subtle floral scent of her perfume mingling with the crisp night air.

"I should go," Beth said softly, though she

made no move to leave. "Early classes tomorrow."

"Of course," Will agreed. "Thank you for tonight. The rehearsal, I mean. It was good to sing again after so long."

"You have a lovely voice," Beth told him, her tone sincere. "Rich and warm baritone. You should sing more often."

The compliment pleased him more than it probably should have. "Only in safe company," he replied with a small smile. "The sheep are my usual audience, and they're not particularly discerning."

Beth laughed, the sound warming his heart. "Well, I'm honoured to provide a more appreciative audience." She opened her car door, then paused. "Goodnight, Will. See you Friday."

"Goodnight, Beth."

As Will drove home, he hummed one of the carols from rehearsal, his mood lighter than it had been in months. The prospect of Friday evening—a relaxed dinner together, the stargazing, simply spending time with Beth away from their various community obligations— filled Will with a happiness he hadn't felt for a long time.

Jon's warning echoed in his memory: *Just be careful, mate.* And Will was being careful, maintaining the 'just friends' boundary that Beth seemed to need. But he couldn't deny that his feelings were deepening beyond friendship into something more complex and potentially risky.

The farm came into view, moonlight silvering the paddocks and outbuildings. Will pulled up to the house, the dogs greeting him with their usual enthusiasm. As he moved through his evening routine—feeding the dogs, checking on the pregnant ewe, making a simple late dinner—his thoughts kept returning to Beth.

Something in her past had wounded her; that much was clear. Something that had made her wary of performance, of putting herself forward, perhaps even of forming close connections. Will had no desire to pry—Beth would share her story if and when she was ready. But he found himself wanting to understand, wanting to help heal whatever hurt she carried.

As he settled into bed that night, a half-formed Christmas carol still playing in his mind, he acknowledged the truth he'd been avoiding: he was falling for Beth Curtis. The sensible course would be to pull back, to protect himself from potential disappointment.

But as he drifted toward sleep, he knew he wouldn't do that. Some risks were worth taking, and getting to know Beth better—helping her find her place in Bindarra Creek, even if that place proved temporary—felt increasingly like one of those risks.

Friday evening couldn't come soon enough.

Chapter Ten

Friday evening arrived clear and crisp, with a sharp bite to the air that promised another frost in the morning. April had quickly moved into May, and now it was the middle of June, with the Christmas in July celebrations coming up very quickly. Will had spent the day splitting his attention between farm tasks and his mind wandering to the evening ahead. He'd checked the weather forecast obsessively, relieved that the skies would remain clear for their stargazing.

As he showered and changed into fresh jeans and a blue button-down shirt that Cleo once told him "brought out his eyes," Will tried to remind himself that this wasn't a date. Just two friends enjoying a meal, and afterwards, the stars. Nothing more complicated than that.

Yet as he drove toward Beth's cottage at precisely six-twenty, allowing for the ten-minute drive to the pub, the flutter of anticipation coiled in Will's stomach. This was different from the festival activities they'd shared—more deliberate, more personal.

Beth's cottage looked welcoming in the early evening light, with a warm glow from the windows and smoke curling from the chimney. Will pulled into the short driveway and took a deep breath before stepping out of the ute. He'd brought a thermos of hot chocolate and extra blankets for the stargazing portion of the evening, tucked behind the seat.

Beth opened the door before he could knock, wrapped in a navy wool coat with a burgundy scarf. Her hair was loose around her shoulders rather than in its usual practical style for school and rehearsals, and Will was momentarily struck by how different—how lovely—she looked outside of her professional persona.

"Right on time," she said with a small smile. "I just need to grab my bag."

Will waited by the door as Beth collected her things, taking in the glimpse of her living space—a piano in the corner of the small sitting room, bookshelves lined with music books and novels, and, surprisingly, a collection of vintage vinyl records in a wooden crate beside a turntable.

"I didn't picture you as a vinyl collector," he

commented as she rejoined him.

Beth's expression brightened. "My grandfather started my collection when I was twelve. Said digital couldn't capture the warmth of real music." She locked the door behind them. "It's one of the few things I made sure to bring with me from Sydney."

The drive to the pub was short but pleasant, their conversation flowing easily about the week's events—the progress of the Christmas play rehearsals, the latest carol practice, Will's pregnant ewe that was now showing definite signs of early lambing.

"I might have to check on her when we get back from stargazing," Will explained. "She's a first-timer and looking restless this afternoon."

"We don't have to do the stargazing if you need to get back to the farm," Beth offered. "I'd understand."

"She'll be fine," Will assured her. "And I wouldn't want you to miss the view from the ridge. It's something special, especially for someone who's lived in the city."

The pub was bustling with its usual Friday night crowd, but they managed to secure a corner table near the fireplace. The menu was simple—pizza, burgers, and hearty pub fare—but the atmosphere was warm and convivial.

"Right, pizza it is," Will said, scanning the options. "I'm thinking something with proper meat on it."

"Pepperoni?" Beth suggested, then wrinkled her nose. "Actually, no. Too greasy."

"Ham and pineapple," Will said decisively.

Beth's eyes widened in mock horror. "Absolutely not. Pineapple does not belong on pizza."

"Says who? It's a perfectly reasonable topping."

"Says anyone with taste buds," Beth countered, leaning back in her chair with an amused smile. "What about chicken?"

Will pulled a face. "Chicken on pizza is just wrong. Chicken belongs on a plate with vegetables, not hiding under cheese pretending to be something it's not."

"You're being ridiculous," Beth laughed, the sound drawing glances from nearby tables. "Chicken is versatile."

"Chicken is for people who can't commit to real pizza toppings," Will shot back. "Like mushrooms. Or proper sausage."

They settled eventually on a compromise—half vegetarian for Beth, half Italian sausage for Will—and ordered a couple of beers. The banter continued as they waited, easy and teasing, until their conversation drifted to other topics.

"The Christmas play is coming along well," Beth said, taking a sip of her beer. "The students are really getting into character now."

"Even Gavin Wang?"

"Especially Gavin Wang. He's decided the innkeeper should have a limp and a Yorkshire accent."

Will chuckled. "Marsha and Chen will be proud. They're on the SES too."

The pizza arrived, and they divided it between them, the conversation flowing easily between bites. It was Beth who eventually grew quieter, her fork pushing a piece of capsicum around her plate.

"This is nice," she said suddenly, looking up at him. "Just... normal conversation. No pressure."

Something in her tone made Will set down his slice. "Pressure?"

"Not have to be someone who isn't me." Beth was quiet for a moment, seeming to think before she spoke. "I had a relationship in Sydney that was... difficult. Everything felt like a performance, like I was constantly being judged on whether I was interesting enough, accomplished enough." She gave a small shrug. "It's refreshing to just talk about sheep and pizza toppings without feeling like I need to impress anyone."

Will felt something tighten in his chest—not jealousy exactly, but a protective instinct he hadn't expected. "Anyone who needed you to perform wasn't worth your time."

"I know that now," Beth said quietly, then brightened. "Anyway, that's in the past. This is much better. I really enjoy your company, Will."

They finished their meal as they chatted, Beth's honesty changing the atmosphere between them—not awkwardly, but with a kind of understanding. When Will insisted on paying the bill as usual Beth didn't argue.

As they walked toward the door, the cool evening air waiting beyond the warm pub, Beth slipped her arm through his—a gesture so natural it caught Will off guard.

"Thank you," she said softly, "for being

such a lovely friend."

The word "friend" should have been reassuring, Will thought, but instead it left him with an odd sense of both comfort and disappointment as they stepped out into the crisp night air.

"Ready for some stargazing?" he asked. "Or are you too tired after a full week?"

"Definitely not too tired," Beth assured him. "I've been looking forward to it. Though I didn't realise how cold it would get after dark."

"I came prepared," Will said, opening the ute door for her. "Extra blankets and hot chocolate in a thermos."

Beth's smile was warm. "You thought of everything."

The drive to Will's property took about fifteen minutes, the road winding out of town and into the countryside. As they turned onto the private track that led to his farm, Will gave Beth a running commentary on the area's history and the neighbouring properties.

"That's the old Lette homestead on the right," he pointed out as they passed a weathered gate. "Have you seen Fig Tree Lodge, where Edwina lives? It's been in their family since they settled here."

"Not yet, but Cleo told me about it." Beth looked out at the shadowy landscape with interest. "How long has your family been here?"

"Since 1923," Will replied. "My great-grandfather bought the place after returning from World War I. It was run-down back then, mostly scrub and rocks. He built it up bit by bit, and each generation has added to it since."

"And now it's just you?" she asked quietly.

"Yep, just me and the dogs."

They crested a hill, and Will pulled off onto a flat area overlooking the valley below. The lights of Bindarra Creek twinkled in the distance, a small island of light in the vast darkness.

"This is it," he said, cutting the engine. "The best view on the property."

They stepped out of the ute, and Beth immediately tilted her head upward, a soft gasp escaping her. Above them, the night sky blazed with stars—not the faint scattering visible in cities, but thousands upon thousands of stars in brilliant clarity, the sweep of the Milky Way a luminous band cutting across the heavens.

"Oh, my goodness. It's incredible," she

breathed. "I've never seen anything like it."

Will smiled, pleased by her reaction. He'd seen this view countless times throughout his life, but Beth's wonder made him see it anew. He spread a thick wool blanket on the grass beside the ute, then retrieved another to wrap around their shoulders if needed. The thermos of hot chocolate and two enamel mugs completed the setup.

"Your grandfather was right about vinyl records," Will said as they settled on the blanket, shoulders almost touching. "Some things are better experienced in their raw form, not digitised or filtered. The stars are like that, too."

Beth looked up at the dark expanse above them. "In Sydney, you'd be lucky to see a dozen stars on a clear night. I've never seen a starry sky like this."

Will poured hot chocolate into the mugs, handing one to Beth. "See that bright patch there?" he pointed. "That's the Southern Cross. And below it, those two bright stars are the Pointers."

"The ones on the Australian flag," Beth nodded. "I recognise those."

"Early navigators used them to find south," Will explained. "My grandfather taught me to use them as a compass when I was a boy. Said I'd never be lost on my own land as long as I could see the stars."

"That's beautiful," Beth said softly. "A tradition passed down." She took a sip of her hot chocolate. "Did your family have other traditions? Christmas ones, maybe? For the play research," she added quickly.

Will smiled, recognising the professional excuse. "We did. Still do, some of them. My grandmother was big on Christmas, even though it falls in summer here. She was English originally, so she brought over traditions that didn't always make sense in the Australian climate."

"Like what?"

"Like insisting on a hot roast dinner even when it was thirty-five degrees outside," Will chuckled. "And making Christmas pudding months in advance, stirring wishes into the mixture. We'd all have to take a turn with the wooden spoon, moving it clockwise and making a wish."

Beth's expression was thoughtful. "That's

lovely. The wishing part, I mean. Maybe we could incorporate something like that into the play—a contrast between English traditions and Australian reality."

"There were Australian traditions too," Will added. "Dad would always cut fresh eucalyptus branches to decorate the house. Said they smelled better than pine. And we'd have cricket matches on the lawn after lunch, the whole extended family playing until sunset."

They fell into conversation about Christmas memories, Beth sharing stories of childhood holidays in Sydney—carols in the park, watching the surf lifesavers dressed as Santa arrive on beaches, the glass pyramid at David Jones department store filled with animated scenes.

"What about your family?" Will asked gently. "Do they still live in Sydney?"

Beth's expression clouded slightly. "My parents moved to the Central Coast a few years ago. We're not... especially close. They never quite understood my choice to pursue music. They're both very practical—Dad's an accountant, Mum's a nurse. They wanted something more stable for me."

"But you found stability in teaching," Will observed.

"Eventually," Beth agreed, her tone suggesting there was more to the story. "Though I did try the performance route first, after the Conservatorium. It didn't work out. When I took up teaching, my parents were happy."

Will sensed they were approaching whatever wound Beth carried, the one that made her shy away from performing despite her obvious talent. He waited, giving her space to continue or change the subject as she chose.

Beth took another sip of her hot chocolate, seeming to gather her thoughts. "David, the one I mentioned at the pub, was another musician," she said finally, her voice measured. "He was more established than I was, with connections in the Sydney music scene. We taught at the same school."

Will remained silent, aware that Beth was sharing something significant.

"He drove a wedge between me and Mum and Dad. And he was very critical of my performing style," she continued. "He always said I was too technical, too controlled. I lacked the emotional connection that makes a true artist. At first, I worked harder, trying to prove him wrong. But gradually, I started to believe him." She looked down at her mug. "By the end, I couldn't perform without hearing his critiques in my head. So, I stopped performing altogether."

"He was wrong," Will said quietly but with conviction.

Beth looked up, surprised by his certainty.

"I've heard you play," Will continued. "When you're working on the arrangements for the play, or demonstrating for the carol singers. Nothing is lacking in your connection to the music. And the students feel it too—they respond to your passion when you teach."

Beth's expression softened with something like wonder. "That's ... thank you. That means a lot."

"What happened?" Will asked gently. "With David?"

A shadow crossed Beth's face. "I found out he'd been having an affair with a student. A senior. She was talented, and he'd been giving her 'private coaching'." The bitterness in her voice was palpable. "When it came out, he somehow twisted things to suggest I'd known about it. The school thought it best if we both left. His reputation recovered faster than mine did."

Will felt a surge of anger on Beth's behalf. "That's why you came to Bindarra Creek."

She nodded. "No school in Sydney would touch me after that, even though I'd done nothing wrong. The rumours were enough. Jaclyn was the only one willing to give me a chance. She knew a former colleague of mine who vouched for me."

"I'm sorry," Will said simply. "You deserved better."

Beth shrugged, attempting nonchalance, though the hurt was still visible. "It worked out, in a way. I'm rebuilding here. The students are wonderful. The town is... growing on me." Her eyes met his briefly. "Some parts more than others."

The moment hung between them. Will was acutely aware of their proximity, of how easy it would be to close the small distance between them. But Beth had just shared a painful confidence, and he sensed that what she needed now was simply acceptance, not romantic complications.

"Look," he said, pointing upward to a streak of light across the sky. "A shooting star."

Beth's face tilted upward, her expression clearing. "Make a wish," she said softly.

Will closed his eyes briefly, his wish already formed in his heart. When he opened them, he found Beth watching him, something unreadable in her expression.

"Thank you," she said.

"For what?"

"For listening. For not judging. For showing me the stars." She gestured to the sky above them. "This is... it helps put things in perspective, somehow. Makes Sydney and David and all that seem very far away."

"That's part of why I love it here," Will admitted. "The land, the sky—they've been here long before us and will be here long after. Makes our troubles seem minute."

A comfortable silence fell between them as they sipped their hot chocolate and gazed at the stars. Will was conscious of a shift in their relationship—a deepening, a new layer of trust established through Beth's confidence and his response to it.

After a while, his phone buzzed in his pocket. Checking it, he saw a text from Jordan: **Ewe looking restless. Might want to check when you get back**.

"Farm duty calls?" Beth asked, noticing his expression.

"My neighbour. Called in on his way home to check up on Sassy for me."

"Sassy?"

"The ewe." Will nodded, feeling silly. "Looks like our expectant mother might be getting closer to delivery."

"I love that she has a name. That tells me a lot about you, Will."

They packed up the blankets and thermos, making their way back to the ute. As Will drove back toward town, Beth seemed thoughtful, looking out at the dark landscape.

"I'd like to learn more about farm life," she said suddenly. "For the colonial Christmas scene in the play," she added. "What would it have been like for those early settlers celebrating Christmas in this landscape?"

Will recognised the request beneath the professional justification. "I'd be happy to show you. The lambing should be starting in earnest in a couple of weeks. It's something special—new life, the cycle continuing. Very different from city experiences."

"I'd like that," Beth said simply.

When they reached her cottage, Will walked her to the door, the night air cold around them. Under the porch light, Beth's face was softly illuminated, her eyes reflecting the warmth of the evening they'd shared.

"Thank you for tonight," she said. "The pizza was fun, but the stars... that was something I'll remember."

"Any time," Will replied. "The viewing spot on the ridge isn't going anywhere."

Beth smiled, then, in a move that surprised him, stepped forward and kissed his cheek lightly. "Goodnight, Will. Good luck with Sassy."

Before he could respond, she had slipped inside, the door closing softly behind her. Will stood for a moment, his hand unconsciously touching the spot where her lips had brushed his skin. Then he turned and walked back to his ute, a smile playing at the corners of his mouth.

As he drove back to the farm, his thoughts were in turmoil. The evening had confirmed what he already knew—that his feelings for Beth were deepening beyond friendship. But her story had also revealed the wounds she still carried, the wariness that made her hesitant to form new attachments.

The sensible course would be to maintain the boundaries of friendship, to respect Beth's need for healing and space. But the warmth of her kiss on his cheek, brief as it was, suggested that perhaps she, too, was feeling the pull between them.

For now, Will decided, he would follow her lead, offering friendship and support, and a connection to Bindarra Creek that might, in time, help her see this place as more than a temporary haven. Whether that led to something deeper between them, only time would tell.

But as the lights of his farmhouse came into view, Will knew that was what he wanted. Because somewhere between building play sets, singing carols, and sharing stars, Beth Curtis had found her way into his heart in a way no one else ever had.

Chapter Eleven

As the warm June sun cast long shadows across the school grounds, Beth gathered her sheet music from the piano in the hall. Another successful rehearsal with the play cast had left her feeling cautiously optimistic. Billy Kendall-Cummings had proven to be a natural as Scrooge, bringing both humour and unexpected depth to the character. The other students were coming along nicely as well, growing more confident with each session. Gavin had decided to take on an Aussie accent, much to her relief.

Two months into her time at Bindarra Creek, Beth was settling into rhythms she hadn't anticipated. Her days were filled with teaching, rehearsals, and an ever-expanding circle of community activities. Between the Christmas in July preparations and the choir, Beth's calendar was fuller than it had been in Sydney. Yet somehow, it felt less draining, more purposeful.

As she locked the music room, Cleo appeared in the corridor, office files balanced precariously in her arms.

"Beth! Just the person I wanted to see," she called. "How's the play coming along?"

"Very well," Beth replied, moving to help Cleo with her load. "Billy's really stepping up as Scrooge, and Kaylee's choreographed a beautiful dance sequence for the Ghost of Christmas Past scene."

"That's wonderful," Cleo beamed. "The whole town's talking about it. I haven't seen such excitement for the play in years."

A small glow of pride filled Beth. "Well, I have excellent material to work with. The students are incredibly talented."

"And they have an excellent director," Cleo added, giving Beth a pointed look. "You've brought something special to the music program. I heard that some of the senior students are suddenly interested in Dickens because of the play."

Beth wasn't quite sure how to respond to the praise. After David's constant criticism, genuine appreciation of her work was not something she accepted easily.

"Speaking of special," Cleo continued, seemingly oblivious to Beth's discomfort, "Will mentioned you're going out to his farm this weekend to see the lambing. Brave choice—farm boots aren't the most glamorous footwear."

Beth smiled, thinking of her newly purchased wellies sitting by her cottage door. "I'm not concerned with glamour. I've never seen a lamb being born. It seems like something I should experience while I'm here."

"And the fact that it's Will's farm has nothing to do with it?" Cleo teased gently.

Beth's cheeks heated. Since their evening stargazing on Will's property two weeks ago, gossip about their relationship had intensified. Despite their careful "just friends" positioning, the town had clearly decided there was more to the story.

"Will's been incredibly helpful with the play sets," Beth said, deliberately focusing on the festival aspect of their relationship. "And he's offered to show me bits of rural life that might inform the colonial Christmas scenes."

Cleo's knowing smile suggested she wasn't fooled. "Of course. Very educational. Well, enjoy the lambing. It's quite something the first time you see it."

"I'm looking forward to meeting Sassy. She

had the first lamb early."

Cleo sent her a long, significant look.

As Beth walked to her car, she found herself both anticipating and apprehensive about the weekend. The evening of stargazing had shifted something between her and Will. His patient listening as she'd shared parts of her story with David, his quiet appreciation of her talents—these had created a crack in the protective walls she'd built around herself.

The brief kiss she'd impulsively placed on his cheek had been an acknowledgment of that shift, a tentative step towards... what, exactly? Beth wasn't sure. She only knew that Will Greaves had become important to her in ways that made her happy and frightened her at the same time.

Saturday morning dawned clear and cool as Beth drove the now-familiar route to Will's property. The winter landscape had a stark beauty—frost-gilded paddocks and fences silhouetted against the pale sky. As she turned onto the long driveway leading to the homestead, that familiar anticipation that seemed to accompany all her interactions with Will lately fluttered in her chest.

He was waiting on the wide verandah of the weatherboard farmhouse, two mugs of steaming coffee in hand. The sight of him—tall and solid in his work clothes, his face lighting up as he saw her car—created a warmth in Beth's chest that had nothing to do with the morning sun.

"Good timing," Will called as she approached. "Coffee before we head out to check on the ewes."

"Perfect," Beth replied, climbing the verandah steps. "I was up late finalising the musical arrangement for the beach Christmas scene. Caffeine is definitely required."

They sat in the soft chairs overlooking the property, sipping their coffee as Will explained the day ahead. Several ewes were expected to lamb, and he needed to check on them regularly. Beth would get to see the process, weather and timing permitting.

"It might be a lot of waiting around," Will warned. "Nature keeps its own schedule."

"I don't mind," Beth assured him. "It's nice to be away from rehearsals and lesson plans for a day."

Will studied her for a moment, his blue-grey eyes thoughtful. "You're looking more relaxed these days. Bindarra Creek agrees with you."

"Does it? I suppose I am settling in better than I thought I would."

"The town's certainly taken to you," Will commented. "Marsha Wang was telling everyone at the SES meeting how brilliantly the play is coming along. Gavin has decided he wants to be the next Chris Hemsworth, and apparently, your modifications to the carols for the parade are 'inspired'."

Beth smiled. "That's kind of her. I'm just doing my job."

"You're doing more than that," Will said quietly. "You're bringing something new to traditions that had become a bit stale. People appreciate it, even if they don't say it directly."

Before Beth could respond, Will's mobile phone buzzed. Checking it, he stood quickly. "One of the ewes in the south paddock is in labour. Perfect timing. Ready to see some lambs being born?"

The morning passed in a blur of activity as Will checked on his flock, paying particular attention to the pregnant ewes. Beth watched, fascinated, as he moved among the animals with calm confidence, his large hands gentle as he examined them. When one ewe went into active labour, Will crouched beside her, murmuring encouragement as she strained.

"She's another first-timer like Sassy," he explained to Beth, who was watching from a respectful distance. "Sometimes they need a bit of help."

The birth itself was messy, intense, and surprisingly quick. Within twenty minutes, a wet, wobbling lamb was taking its first breaths, while its mother licked it clean. Beth found herself unexpectedly moved by the simple miracle of it—new life emerging into the world with Will as its gentle guardian.

"That's amazing," she breathed, watching the lamb struggle to stand on spindly legs.

Will smiled, his expression content. "Never gets old, seeing them take their first steps. This one's a female. She'll join the breeding flock in a couple of years."

They moved on to check other paddocks, Will explaining the cycle of farm life as they went—the breeding season, lambing, shearing, the careful stewardship of both animals and land that had sustained his family for generations. Beth listened, asking questions, gradually understanding Will's deep connection to this place.

After a simple lunch of bread and cheese on the verandah, they sat in companionable silence, watching the distant paddocks where new lambs wobbled beside their mothers.

"Thank you for today," Beth said finally. "It's been... wonderful. I've never seen that side of rural life before."

"Most city people haven't," Will replied. "They see the romantic version in films or the economic version in news reports. The reality is somewhere in between—beautiful but hard, rewarding but exhausting."

"You love it, though," Beth observed. It wasn't a question.

"I do," Will nodded. "It's more than a job. It's a way of life, a connection to something larger than myself." He glanced at her, his expression curious. "What about you? What connects you that deeply?"

The question caught Beth off guard, though she knew the answer immediately. "Music. Even when it was painful, even when David..." She trailed off, the familiar knot forming in her throat.

"Forget him, Beth. Let go of the lack of confidence. Anyone who's seen you working with the students or the carol singers knows that. You connect deeply with the music and with the people you're teaching. It's obvious in every interaction you have."

The certainty in his words brought unexpected tears to Beth's eyes. She blinked them away quickly, embarrassed by the emotion. "Thank you. That means a lot, coming from you."

Will looked slightly puzzled. "Why from me specifically?"

Beth considered the question, searching for the right words. "Because you're... honest. You don't say things you don't mean. At least, that's how you seem to me."

A slow smile spread across Will's face, reaching his eyes and warming them. "That might be the nicest thing anyone's said to me."

Their eyes met and held, and Beth reached out and put her hand on his forearm.

The moment was interrupted by the distant ringing of Will's mobile phone. He grimaced apologetically. "Sorry. Excuse me a moment."

As he stepped into the house to take the call,

Beth gazed out at the peaceful landscape, feeling more settled in herself than she had in months. Something was healing about this place, about the steady rhythm of farm life that Will had described. Perhaps that was part of his appeal—how grounded he was, the certainty of purpose that seemed to anchor him.

Will returned, looking slightly harried. "Sorry about that. One of the boundary fences is down in the west paddock. I need to fix it before the sheep find their way through."

"I should probably head back to town anyway," Beth said, standing. "I promised Billy I'd work with him on the final monologue tomorrow afternoon."

As she was about to get in the car, Will touched her arm lightly, his expression suddenly less certain. "Before you go—I was wondering if you might be interested in going to Meg and Jack's wedding next Saturday? The ceremony is at Meg's grandmother's museum."

The invitation caught Beth by surprise. A wedding was definitely more personal than their previous outings. "As... friends?" she asked cautiously. "And I don't know them."

Will nodded, though something flickered in

his eyes. "Of course. But it should be a nice event. The whole town will be there, so it doesn't matter if you haven't met them yet. and the reception's at the Riverside Pub afterwards. Good food, music, dancing if you're inclined."

Beth hesitated only briefly. Despite her reservations about getting too personally involved in Bindarra, the prospect of attending the wedding with Will was undeniably appealing. "I'd like that," she said finally. "Thank you for the invitation."

Will's smile brightened considerably. "Great. I'll pick you up at eleven. The ceremony's at noon."

"Eleven is perfect," Beth agreed, a flutter of anticipation already building at the thought of the event.

Chapter Twelve

Will adjusted his tie for the third time, frowning at his reflection in the bedroom mirror. The charcoal suit—purchased two years ago for a cousin's wedding in Armidale—felt stiff and unfamiliar after months of farm clothes and casual wear. But Meg and Jack's wedding called for proper attire, and Will was determined to make an effort.

Especially since Beth would be his companion for the day.

He'd been careful to frame the invitation as a friendly outing, conscious of Beth's caution about forming attachments. But in the privacy of his own thoughts, Will acknowledged that this felt different from their previous activities together. More like a proper date, with all the anticipation and nervousness that entailed.

Beth's openness during her visit to the farm had touched him deeply. Her willingness to share the full story of David's betrayal suggested a growing trust between them, a letting down of the protective barriers she'd maintained since arriving in Bindarra. And when he'd overheard her singing in the school hall—her voice pure and expressive, filled with the very emotion David had claimed she lacked—Will had felt a surge of both admiration and anger. Admiration for her undeniable talent, and anger at the man who had nearly convinced her to silence it.

The memory of Beth's voice, of the unguarded moment before she'd realised he was listening, stayed with Will as he made final preparations for the day. He'd cut fresh flowers from his mother's garden at the edge of the property—native blooms that would complement Beth's colouring, arranged simply in brown paper and twine. Not too romantic, he hoped, but a gesture of appreciation nonetheless.

As Will drove toward Beth's cottage, he found himself uncharacteristically nervous. He'd known Beth for two months now, had worked alongside her on various festival preparations, and had shared conversations both casual and deep. Yet today felt significant, a potential turning point in whatever was developing between them.

Beth was waiting on her small front porch, and the sight of her momentarily stilled Will's breath. She wore a simple long-sleeved dress in a pale blue that complemented her dark hair, which fell in loose waves around her shoulders rather than in its usual practical style. She looked beautiful, but more than that—she looked relaxed, at ease in a way Will hadn't seen before.

"Right on time," she smiled as Will approached, the flowers in hand. "And you've brought half the garden, I see."

Will felt himself blushing slightly. "Just a few natives from Mum's garden plot. Thought you might like them."

Beth accepted the bouquet, her expression softening as she inhaled their subtle fragrance. "They're lovely. Thank you, Will. Let me put them in water before we go."

As they drove to Mary Moonie's Museum at the edge of town, conversation flowed easily between them. Beth shared stories of the week's rehearsals, including a minor crisis when Billy temporarily lost his voice and had to whisper his way through Scrooge's most dramatic scene.

"Poor kid was devastated," she laughed.

"But his whispered version was actually quite effective—added a vulnerability to the character that worked surprisingly well."

Will enjoyed the animation in her face as she spoke about the students, the affection and pride evident in her voice. It was another side of Beth that had gradually emerged as she settled into Bindarra—the passionate teacher, invested in her students' development both musically and personally.

Mary Moonie's Museum was a reconstructed homestead on the outskirts of Bindarra Creek, named for one of the region's pioneering women. The building and its surrounding gardens had been lovingly restored by the historical society and now served as both a museum and a venue for special events. Today, the gardens were transformed with chairs arranged in rows facing an arch twined with native flowers and eucalyptus leaves.

As they joined the gathering guests, Will and Beth were greeted warmly by various townspeople. Will noted with satisfaction how many people now addressed Beth by name, including her in conversations about town matters beyond the festival. She was no longer simply "the new music teacher" but Beth, a recognised and valued community member.

The ceremony itself was simple but moving. Will was acutely aware of Beth beside him, of her emotional response to the couple's obvious devotion. When their hands accidentally brushed during a particularly touching moment in the vows, neither pulled away immediately.

After the ceremony, as photographs were being taken and champagne circulated among the guests, Will and Beth found themselves speaking with Tessa Myers from the Fig Tree Lodge.

"You've done wonders with the play rehearsals, Beth," Tessa commented. "Kaylee can't stop talking about it. Says it's the best production they've ever done."

Beth smiled, accepting the praise with growing confidence. "The students are incredibly talented. And Will's sets have made all the difference."

"You two make a good team," Tessa observed with a knowing glance between them. "Complementary strengths."

Will felt Beth tense slightly beside him, wary of the implication. "We've enjoyed collaborating on various festival projects," he said diplomatically. "Beth's brought fresh ideas to traditions that needed revitalising."

The conversation turned to other festival preparations, but Will remained conscious of Beth's subtle retreat, the slight distance she maintained after Tessa's comment. Even after two months in Bindarra, she remained cautious about being linked too closely with him in public conversation.

The reception at the Riverside Pub was in full swing by mid-afternoon. The historic stone building overlooking the river had been decorated with fairy lights and flowers, creating a festive atmosphere despite clouds building in the south that threatened rain later. Tables spilled from the main dining room onto the covered deck, where a local band set up for dancing.

Will and Beth were seated with Mark and Leah, along with the Kendalls. Conversation flowed easily, lubricated by good food and excellent local wines. Will noticed Beth gradually relaxing again, laughing at Jon's stories about SES rescues and contributing her anecdotes about city life.

"I'm still adjusting to how everyone knows everything here," she admitted when the topic turned to small-town living. "In Sydney, I could go weeks without speaking to my neighbours. Here, the girls at the café know what I bought at the supermarket before I've even unpacked it."

"It takes some getting used to," Leah agreed sympathetically. "When I first moved here from Sydney, I found it suffocating. Now I can't imagine living anywhere else. There's something to be said for being known, being part of a community."

"Even with the gossip?" Beth asked, a hint of her lingering reservations evident in her tone.

"Especially with the gossip," Cleo laughed. "It's like a free security system. Nothing happens in Bindarra without someone noticing."

As the meal concluded and the band began to play, couples drifted toward the dance floor. The music was a mix of standards and contemporary songs, skilfully adapted for dancing by the four-piece band. Will watched as Meg and Jack took the floor for their first dance, their faces alight with joy as they moved together.

Beth seemed thoughtful, harking back to the earlier conversation. "It's not always easy, is it? Choosing to move from the city to a small town."

Will recognised the underlying question—Beth was considering her future, still uncertain about whether Bindarra could be more than a temporary haven. "No," he agreed. "But sometimes the choice makes itself. You find yourself becoming part of a place before you've consciously decided to stay."

Their eyes met, and Will saw understanding in Beth's gaze—she recognised that he meant her gradual integration into Bindarra Creek life. Before she could respond, the band shifted to a slow, romantic standard, and couples around them moved to the dance floor.

Will hesitated only briefly before extending his hand. "Would you care to dance?"

Beth's momentary pause reflected her internal calculation—the step this represented, the blurring of the "just friends" boundary they'd maintained. Then she smiled and placed her hand in his. "I'd love to."

The dance floor was crowded enough to provide a certain anonymity as Will led Beth into a simple waltz step. She moved gracefully, following his lead with natural rhythm. The physical proximity was new—Beth's hand in his, his other hand at the small of her back, their bodies moving in harmony with the music and each other.

"I didn't know you could dance," Beth said, looking up at him with surprise and something warmer.

"Farm boys have hidden talents," Will replied with a smile. "Mum insisted on proper lessons when I was a teenager. Said no son of hers would stomp on girls' toes at school dances."

Beth laughed, the sound brightening her face. "I like that she did that. A woman after my own heart." She seemed to catch herself, a flash of vulnerability crossing her face.

Will pretended not to notice, keeping the conversation light as they continued to dance. But he was intensely aware of Beth gradually relaxing in his arms, of the trust in her willingness to follow his lead. By the third song, she seemed to have forgotten her self-consciousness, moving with him as if they'd danced together for years.

Night had settled but inside, however, the atmosphere was warm and happy, the lights glowing more golden as the afternoon light faded. Will guided Beth through another slow dance, hyperaware of her hand in his, the subtle floral scent of her perfume, the way her hair brushed his cheek when they turned.

As the song drew to a close, they were at the edge of the dance floor, partially sheltered by a large potted plant. In the semi-privacy of the moment, with the music fading and Beth still in his arms, Will felt an almost overwhelming urge to kiss her. Their eyes met, and he saw something in her expression—a mixture of desire and hesitation, of wanting and fearing.

Will began to lower his head slowly, giving her time to pull away if she chose. Beth's lips parted slightly, her eyes darkening. The moment stretched between them…

A loud bang startled them both. Beth stepped back quickly, her cheeks flushed, expression a mixture of relief and regret.

Will turned around. "It's okay, someone knocked one of the high tables near the door into the glass. Nothing's broken."

But the moment was gone.

"I should..." Beth gestured vaguely toward the restrooms. "I'll be right back."

Will nodded, letting her go, aware that they'd reached some kind of threshold. The almost-kiss hung between them, an acknowledgment of feelings that had been developing for weeks.

By the time Beth returned, the dance floor had transformed into a lively celebration. The moment for quiet intimacy had passed, but something had shifted nonetheless. As they rejoined the festivities, Will noticed Beth maintained a slight physical distance, careful not to repeat the closeness they'd shared during the slow dances.

The celebration continued unabated, the mix of music and laughter creating its own joyful storm.

As the night drew to a close and some guests began to depart, Will and Beth sat outside at a small table on the covered deck, watching the moonlight on the river while sipping coffee.

"Quite a day," Will commented, deliberately keeping his tone casual.

Beth was quiet, and she lifted a hand to cover her mouth s she yawned. "Sorry, it's been a big week."

"We should probably head home soon," Will suggested, checking his watch.

Beth nodded agreement, and they quickly made their farewells, joining other guests who were heading for their cars.

"My first country wedding," she commented as Will started the engine. "And I loved it."

The drive back to Beth's cottage was companionable if slightly subdued. As they pulled up outside her home, she smiled at him.

"Thank you for the lift. And thank you for inviting me to go with you."

"I'll walk you to the door," Will said.

"You don't have to—" Beth began to protest.

"I insist," Will interrupted gently. "My mother raised me with certain standards."

This drew a smile from Beth, and she waited as Will came around to her side and opened the door. The short walk to her door was silent, both of them acutely aware of the earlier moment of almost-intimacy.

At her doorstep, Beth turned to face him, her expression thoughtful in the dim porch light. "Thank you for today, Will. It was... special."

"It was," Will agreed, choosing his words carefully. "I'm pleased you came with me."

They stood for a moment, looking out over the paddock that ran along the side of the cottage.

Will knew he could try again—lean forward, close the distance between them, finish what had begun on the dance floor. But Beth's earlier hesitance stayed with him, and he knew she needed time to process her feelings.

"Good night, Beth," he said finally, taking a deliberate step back. "I'll see you at the karaoke night?"

Relief and something like disappointment flickered across her face. "Yes. Good night, Will. Drive safely, and thank you again."

He waited until she was safely inside before returning to his ute. As he drove home through, he replayed the day in his mind. The almost-kiss had been a moment of truth, revealing feelings that couldn't be disguised as mere friendship. But Beth wasn't ready—he knew that.

The question was why? Was it still too soon after her ex? Was she still uncertain about her future in Bindarra Creek? Or was he imagining her interest?

Will had no answers, only the certainty of his growing feelings for Beth Curtis. Today had confirmed what he'd suspected for weeks—that she was becoming very important to him.

Some risks were worth taking, even knowing the potential for disappointment.

And Beth Curtis, Will reflected as he drifted toward sleep, was definitely worth the risk.

Chapter Thirteen

Beth stood at the back of the school hall, watching as the students ran through the final scene of the Christmas play. Billy Kendall-Cummings, had fully recovered from his bout of laryngitis. Kaylee Miller moved gracefully as the Ghost of Christmas Past, her dance training evident in every gesture. The colonial Christmas scene, enhanced by Will's beautifully crafted set pieces, had come together perfectly.

"And... scene!" Beth called as the music faded. "That was excellent, everyone. Billy, wonderful emotional range. Kaylee, beautiful movement. Gillian, your timing on the Christmas Present entrance is perfect."

The students beamed under her praise, their pride in the production evident. Even Eddie Taylor and Gavin Wang, initially the most reluctant participants, were now fully engaged in their roles.

"One more full run-through on Wednesday, then dress rehearsal on Friday," Beth reminded them as they gathered their belongings.

"Opening night is just over a week away, so make sure you're practising your lines and songs at home."

As the students filed out, chattering excitedly about the upcoming performance, Beth gathered her score sheets and notes. The play had evolved beyond her initial expectations, becoming something she was proud of. The students had embraced her vision, bringing enthusiasm and talent to what could have been a routine school production.

The door at the back of the hall opened, and Beth looked up to see Violet entering, her copper hair gleaming in the afternoon light.

"Caught the end of rehearsal," Violet said, approaching the piano where Beth was organising her music. "It's looking fantastic, Beth. Those kids are going to knock everyone's socks off."

"They're working really hard," Beth agreed, unable to suppress a smile of pride. "And having proper sets has made all the difference."

"Will's handiwork," Violet nodded, a knowing glint in her eye. "Speaking of your farmer friend, how was the wedding? Was it properly romantic? Did you dance under the stars?"

Beth felt herself blushing at the memory of Will's arms around her, the almost-kiss that had both thrilled and terrified her. "It was a lovely ceremony," she said, deliberately focusing on safer aspects of the day.

"And?" Violet prompted, clearly expecting more.

"And... we danced," Beth admitted. "Will's surprisingly good at it."

"I bet he is," Violet grinned. "Those farmer hands are good for all sorts of things. So, are you finally admitting this is more than friendship?"

Beth busied herself with her sheet music, avoiding Violet's perceptive gaze. "It's complicated, Vi."

"Only because you're making it complicated," Violet replied, perching on the edge of the piano bench. "It's obvious you like him. And he's clearly smitten with you. What's holding you back?"

The question hung in the air, demanding an answer that Beth wasn't sure she could answer even to herself. The almost-kiss at the wedding had forced her to confront feelings she'd been trying to ignore—attraction, yes, but also fear. Fear of being vulnerable again, of trusting someone with her heart after David's betrayal. Fear of committing to something in a place she'd only ever intended as a temporary refuge.

"I'm not staying in Bindarra forever," she said finally, voicing one of her concerns. "This was always meant to be a stepping stone, a place to rebuild my reputation before moving to a larger school in Newcastle or Armidale."

"Was?" Violet caught the past tense. 'So that's changed?"

Beth sighed, acknowledging the uncertainty that had been growing within her. "I don't know, Vi. I came here with such clear plans— keep my head down, rebuild my professional credentials, then move on to somewhere with more opportunities. But now..."

"Now you've made connections," Violet finished for her. "You've put down roots without intending to."

"Something like that," Beth agreed. "The students, the play, the festival—I'm invested in it all now. And it's not just professional. I care about this place, the people."

"Including Will," Violet added gently.

Beth nodded, finally meeting her friend's gaze. "Especially Will," she admitted. "He's... different from anyone I've known. Steady, genuine, perceptive. Being with him feels..." She searched for the right word. "Safe. But not in a boring way. In a way that makes me feel I can be myself."

"That sounds a lot like falling in love to me," Violet observed.

"That's what scares me," Beth confessed. "After my ex, I swore I wouldn't let myself be that vulnerable again. And with Will, the stakes seem even higher somehow."

"Because he's the real deal," Violet said simply.

Beth considered this, recognising the truth in Violet's words. "At the wedding, we almost... there was a moment when..." She couldn't quite bring herself to say it.

"You almost kissed," Violet supplied. "And you panicked."

"I didn't panic exactly," Beth protested. "I just needed a moment to think. And then the moment passed, and..." She shrugged helplessly.

"Well, you'll have another chance at the

karaoke night on Friday."

Beth was grateful for the change of subject, even as her mind registered the implications of another evening spent with Will in a social setting. "I'm not sure if I'll go."

" It's six-thirty for dinner at the pub before the karaoke starts at seven-thirty," Violet replied, standing. "And Beth? No overthinking. Be there and just enjoy being with him."

As Violet departed with a wave, Beth finished gathering her materials, her friend's advice echoing in her mind. No overthinking—easier said than done for someone whose overthinking had become a protective mechanism after David's betrayal.

The days leading up to the karaoke night were consumed with play rehearsals, carol practice, and final preparations for the parade. Beth threw herself into her tasks for the rest of the week, finding refuge in the comfort zone of music and teaching. But Will was always there in her mind, and if she was honest, creeping into her heart.

The weather remained unsettled all week, with intermittent rain and persistent cloud cover. .

When Friday evening arrived, Beth stood before her wardrobe, uncharacteristically indecisive about what to wear. It was cold and wet outside. The night was casual, but she still wanted to look nice. After several changes, she settled on dark jeans, a soft blue sweater that complemented her colouring, and low-heeled boots. Her hair, usually pulled back for teaching, was loose around her shoulders.

The Riverside Pub was already bustling when Beth arrived, the Friday evening crowd a mix of locals and tourists drawn by the Christmas in July festivities. She spotted Will immediately, his tall figure easily visible as he stood near the bar, chatting with Joe Rossiter. Something in her chest tightened at the sight of him, a feeling that had become increasingly familiar.

Will looked up as if sensing her presence, his face brightening when he saw her. He said something to Joe, then made his way through the crowd to meet her.

"Beth, hi there." He smiled warmly. "You look lovely."

"Thank you," she replied, feeling the familiar flush of pleasure at his compliment.

"I'm a bit late. Rehearsal ran over—the beach Christmas scene still needs some fine-tuning."

"No worries. Violet's just arrived too, and Joe and I had a beer together while we waited. We've got a table in the back corner, further away from the singing." He smiled down at her. "Unless you want to enter?

"No way. I don't like karaoke. It's a bit embarrassing when people who can't sing put themselves up there."

Will placed his hand lightly on her lower back as he guided her through the crowded pub, the casual touch sending warmth spreading through her. Since the wedding, there had been a subtle shift in their physical interactions—small touches that lingered, a new awareness of each other's proximity.

Violet and Joe were already seated at the table, deep in conversation. Violet looked up as Beth approached, her knowing smile suggesting she'd noted the placement of Will's hand.

The pub had grown increasingly crowded, the atmosphere festive as Christmas music played between the performances. Outside, the promised storm was gathering force, occasional flashes of lightning visible through the windows.

"It's good to have the power back on," Joe commented when they were settled. "That was a corker of a storm on Sunday night."

"It was lucky that it stayed away until after the wedding," Will said. 'My power's still out. What about yours, Joe?'

"It's on and off."

"Same in town. It came back on Wednesday afternoon, but we've had the odd outage since then." Beth leaned forwards, and her hand brushed against Will's. Unlike the wedding, where such contact had made her tense with uncertainty, she found herself appreciating the brief touch, even allowing her fingers to linger against his for a moment. Will's eyes met hers, warm with approval.

The evening unfolded pleasantly as they ordered dinner and drinks, falling into easy conversation about the upcoming festival events. As the karaoke began, Beth initially tensed at the first performer—a local shearer attempting *My Way* with enthusiastic off-key passion. But by the third act, a Year Nine boy from the high school performed a death metal version of *Sweet Caroline,* she was leaning into

Will's shoulder, tears of laughter streaming down her face.

"That was..." she gasped, wiping her eyes, "absolutely terrible."

"Magnificently terrible," Will agreed, enjoying the way she'd relaxed against him.

Another painfully earnest rendition had Beth in fits again. She turned to Will, her eyes bright with mischief and challenge.

"I thought you didn't enjoy karaoke," he said with a wide grin.

"I need to hear someone who can sing! You're much better than that," she said, nodding toward the stage. "Go on, I dare you."

Will raised an eyebrow. "You're daring me to sing karaoke?"

"I am. Unless you're chicken."

Will stood up, shaking his head with a smile. "You'll regret this."

He made his way to the small stage and scrolled through the song list, finally settling on *Make You Feel My Love*. As the opening chords played, the room quieted. Will's voice, warm and steady, filled the pub as his eyes found Beth's across the room and stayed there.

The crowd erupted when he finished, several

locals clapping him on the back as he made his way back to the table. Beth sat perfectly still, her cheeks flushed, not knowing how to react.

"Well done," she said softly, and leaned over to kiss his cheek.

The moment was interrupted by a loud bang, followed immediately by the lights flickering and then going out completely. The pub was plunged into darkness.

"No worries, folks," called the MC, his voice calm in the darkness. "The generator should kick in momentarily. Just stay where you are."

True to his word, emergency lighting came on seconds later, casting the pub in a dim, atmospheric glow. The music system remained silent, however, and the kitchen announced it was closing early due to the power situation.

"That storm created some chaos this week. The power's been unreliable," Beth commented. "Rehearsals have suffered."

"Looks like the night's over," Violet said when the lights stayed off. "We'll head home, I think."

The pub was emptying quickly as other patrons decided to call it a night.

Beth and Will said goodbye to Joe and Violet and headed to Will's ute.

They drove in companionable silence for a while, the quiet creating a strangely intimate atmosphere in the cab of the ute. Beth found herself stealing glances at Will's profile, admiring the quiet competence with which he handled the challenging conditions.

"You're staring," he observed with a small smile, not taking his eyes off the road.

Heat rose in her cheeks. "Just appreciating your driving skills," she said lightly. "We city folk aren't used to navigating country roads."

Will chuckled. "This isn't a country road, you goose. You live in town."

When they finally reached Beth's cottage, Will pulled into her driveway and parked behind her small sedan, before he turned to face her.

"I'll walk you to the door," he said.

"You don't have to—" Beth began to protest.

"I insist," Will interrupted gently.

When they reached the covered porch, Beth turned to face Will.

"Thank you for the ride," she said, suddenly

shy. "And for your performance. You were by far the best. I'm sure you would have won if the power hadn't gone out."

"Thank you. I enjoyed singing that song," Will agreed, his expression warm in the dim porch light. The sky had cleared and the moonlight illuminated Will's face—his blue-grey eyes watching her with a mixture of affection and restraint. He wasn't pushing, wasn't pressuring her. But the attraction between them was palpable, had been growing steadily since their dance at the wedding, perhaps even before.

"I'm not very good at this," she began hesitantly.

"At what?" Will asked, though his eyes suggested he knew exactly what she meant.

"At... letting people get close. At trusting my own judgment. After David—"

"I'm not David," Will interrupted gently. "And I'd never ask you to be anything other than exactly who you are."

The simple sincerity in his voice moved something deep within Beth. Before she could overthink it, she stepped forward and hugged him, burying her face briefly against his chest.

Will's arms came around her, strong and steady, holding her with a tenderness that made her throat tight with emotion.

"Thank you," she whispered, not entirely sure what she was thanking him for—his patience, his understanding, his consistent kindness.

They stood like that for a long moment. When Beth finally stepped back, she saw something in Will's eyes that both thrilled and frightened her—a depth of feeling that couldn't be disguised as mere friendship.

"Good night, Will," she said softly, reaching for her door key.

"Good night, Beth," he replied, his voice equally soft. "I'll see you at the parade tomorrow?"

"I'll be there," she promised. "My students are counting on me."

Will nodded, then hesitated briefly before leaning forward and pressing a gentle kiss to her cheek. "Sweet dreams," he murmured, then turned and walked back to his ute.

"You drive safely. Message me when you get home." Beth watched him go, her hand unconsciously touching the spot where his lips had brushed her skin. The gesture had been simple, almost chaste, yet it had sent warmth spreading through her that had nothing to do with embarrassment.

As Beth prepared for bed, a strange calm settled over her. She knew something was shifting; a gradual acceptance of feelings she'd been trying to deny.

She was falling for Will Greaves. Had been falling, perhaps, since their first meeting at the CWA gathering, or during the quiet evenings working on play sets, or while watching him tenderly tend to newborn lambs.

As Beth drifted toward sleep, lulled by the quiet that was so different to the noise of the city, she found her thoughts turning to tomorrow's parade—another milestone in the festival preparations that had brought her and Will together. Her students would be performing the carols they'd practised for weeks, and Will would be there on the school float playing the piano.

Will's patient approach—his willingness to let her set the pace, to give her the space she needed to trust again—was exactly what she needed to find her way forward.

Chapter Fourteen

Will rose before dawn on parade day, his mind already running through the final preparations for the SES float. He was still assisting with that, even though he was playing the music on the school float. The storm had passed overnight, leaving behind a clear sky and saturated ground. He'd checked the creek levels after he'd texted Beth to say he was safely home—and his power was restored—and the forecast promised a dry day for the festivities.

Roman had called late the previous night, confirming that all was ready: the SES truck was decorated, and the team was psyched to lift the school piano onto the school float.

As Will made his morning coffee, he thought about Beth. The moment on her porch last night—her unexpected hug, the vulnerability in her eyes and the soft warmth of her cheek beneath his lips—had stayed with him all night. He was sure she was getting closer to him.

Today would be busy for both of them.

Beth's students were performing carols at several points along the parade route, while Will played the piano. He'd be beside her for the whole parade.

By mid-morning, Will was at the SES shed, where final preparations for the parade were underway.

"Looking good, isn't it?" Roman said, approaching Will with a clipboard in hand. "The RFS will have a hard time beating us this year."

The assembly point for the parade was at Fred's Garage at the eastern end of the main street. By eleven-thirty, the area was transformed into an organised chaos of floats, community groups, and excited participants. The Lette family's historical float was already positioned near the front, with Natalie and Edwina in period costume, arranging props. The SES float was nearby, and the school float was towards the back.

Will spotted Beth across the crowded assembly area, surrounded by a group of students in matching red and green T-shirts. She was making adjustments to a portable sound system, her attention fully focused on the task.

Even from a distance, Will could see the change in her since her arrival in Bindarra—the confidence in her posture, the easy authority with which she directed the students, the occasional smile that lit her face as she interacted with them.

As if sensing his gaze, Beth looked up, her eyes finding his through the crowd. She raised a hand in greeting, a smile spreading across her face that sent warmth through Will's chest. He hurried across and jumped up on the truck, and sat at the piano that had been lifted there by eight men half an hour ago.

"I'm here, Miss," he said with a wide smile.

Tessa Myers, the parade coordinator, moved through the assembly area with purpose, clipboard in hand and a headset connecting her to volunteers positioned along the route. She paused at the school float, checking it against her list. "Love the piano on board. Good to see you helping the school out, Will." Her smile was knowing.

As noon approached, the various floats and groups began to arrange themselves in the correct order. The SES volunteers, now in full uniform with the addition of Santa hats, were in front of the school float and gathered around for final instructions.

"Remember, this is about community engagement," Roman reminded them. "Wave to the crowds, and keep an eye out for any safety issues along the route. And no using the sirens unless there's an actual emergency," he added with a pointed look at Jon Kendall, who had notoriously misused this privilege at a fundraising event last year.

From his position atop the school float, Will had a good view of the assembly area. Beth was leading her students toward their first performance position. She looked beautiful in a festive red dress with a white cardigan, her dark hair caught up in a simple style with a few loose curls. As she looked across, their eyes met again, and Will raised his hand in a small salute. Beth's answering smile contained something new—a warmth and openness that hadn't been there before, even when tempered by the professional demeanour she maintained in front of her students.

At precisely noon, the town's marching band struck up 'Jingle Bell Rock' with their unique arrangement, and the parade began to move. The atmosphere was festive, with hundreds of locals and tourists lining the main street despite the muddy conditions left by the previous night's storm. Businesses had decorated their storefronts with fairy lights and Christmas themes, and many shops offered special parade-day discounts to draw in the tourists who had come for the festival.

The floats moved smoothly along the street, the various decorations drawing appreciative comments from the crowds. Beth's students' clear young voices rose in a well-rehearsed medley of Australian Christmas songs.

The school float slowed as it passed the performance area; Will stopped playing for a moment as he got a perfect view of Beth conducting her singers. She moved with grace and confidence, drawing the best from each student with subtle gestures and encouraging smiles. The crowd responded enthusiastically to the performance, with many joining in the choruses of 'Six White Boomers' and 'Christmas Where the Gum Trees Grow.'

As the parade continued its slow progress along Main Street, Will looked for Beth at each performance station, smiling at the way she had transformed a group of teenagers into disciplined, enthusiastic performers. By the time they reached the showground at the end of the route, where the parade would conclude and the festival activities would continue, his pride in her accomplishments was matched only by his growing anticipation of standing beside her.

The showground had been transformed for the occasion, with craft displays showing Christmas decorations from around the world, and a central area where the various floats were positioned for final viewing before being dismantled. Beth's carol singers gave their final performance on a small stage near the entrance, gathering their largest audience yet as parade participants and spectators congregated in the festive atmosphere.

Will helped position the SES truck in its designated area, then assisted with safety measures as children were allowed to climb aboard for photos. Between helping youngsters up and down from the vehicle and explaining the star-themed decorations to interested onlookers, he kept glancing toward the performance area, waiting for Beth to finish her official duties.

When the carol performance concluded, the students dispersed to enjoy the festival, and Will finally spotted her making her way through the crowd. She looked tired but happy, her professional responsibilities completed successfully. Will extricated himself from a conversation about bushfire preparedness and moved to intercept her.

"Your singers were brilliant," he said as he reached her, admiration in his voice. "Especially that arrangement of 'Carol of the Birds'—I've never heard it quite like that before."

Beth's face lit up. "Thank you! That was my own arrangement. I wanted something that highlighted the Australian elements without losing the traditional melody."

"Well, it worked beautifully," Will assured her. "How are you holding up? You've been on your feet for hours."

"I'm better than I expected," Beth admitted. "There's something satisfying about seeing the students perform so well after all their preparation."

Will nodded understanding. "The parade float was the same—months of planning coming together in one afternoon. Feels good to see it finished."

"And it looked amazing," Beth told him, her eyes warm with appreciation. "The decorations were fabulous."

They began walking together through the festival grounds, naturally falling into step together. Will smiled when Beth put her arm through his. Around them, the atmosphere was festive and relaxed, with families and children participating in various activities.

"Today has been a huge success," Beth observed, looking around at the crowded showground. "Tessa must be thrilled. She told me they've had record numbers of tourists this year."

"The festival committee took a risk expanding it this year," Will agreed. "But it's paid off. The cooking classes were a big hit, and the movie screenings brought in visitors from as far as Armidale."

"And the play's still to come," Beth added, a mixture of anticipation and nervousness crossing her face. "Final dress rehearsal tomorrow, then opening night on Wednesday."

"The students are more than ready," Will

assured her, recognising the anxiety beneath her words. "And the sets look fantastic, if I do say so myself."

This drew a laugh from Beth. "They do, don't they? Billy was telling me how much he appreciates the details in the colonial scene—said it helps him get into character when he's playing young Scrooge."

Their conversation flowed easily as they ate; Will was acutely aware of a subtle shift in Beth's demeanour—a new openness, a willingness to share her thoughts and feelings without that careful guardedness that had marked their earlier interactions.

As they finished their meal, the festival activities were beginning to wind down for families with young children, though the evening program of music and entertainment would continue for several hours more. The late afternoon sun cast a golden light over the showground, creating a warm, almost magical atmosphere.

"Want to explore the craft tent before it gets crowded again?" Will suggested. "I hear Edwina's historical Christmas display is quite something."

Beth nodded, and they made their way toward the large marquee where local artisans had arranged displays of Christmas crafts and decorations. Inside, the tent was arranged like a journey through Christmas traditions around the world, with sections dedicated to different cultural interpretations of the holiday.

As they moved through the displays, Will found himself watching Beth as much as the exhibits. Her genuine interest in the different traditions, her thoughtful comments on the craftsmanship, her delight in discovering unexpected connections between cultures—all revealed aspects of her character that continued to draw him to her.

At Edwina's historical display, they paused to examine a collection of vintage Christmas cards and decorations from the early days of Bindarra Creek. The oldest items dated back to the 1890s, carefully preserved by generations of the Lette family.

"It's remarkable how some traditions endure," Beth said softly, examining a hand-painted card showing native flowers arranged in the shape of a Christmas tree. "Even when transplanted to a completely different environment."

"People bring their memories with them when they move," Will replied, thinking of his own family's traditions. "They adapt them to new surroundings, but keep the essence of what matters."

Beth's eyes met his, something deeper than casual interest in her expression. "Is that what you think I'm doing here? Adapting to new surroundings while keeping what matters?"

The question caught Will off guard with its directness. "I think," he said carefully, "that you're finding your own way forward. Taking what works from your past and creating something new that suits who you are now."

Beth's expression softened, and in the golden light filtering through the tent, Will was struck again by how beautiful she was—not just physically, but in the quiet strength she'd demonstrated throughout her time in Bindarra Creek, the resilience with which she'd rebuilt her confidence after David's betrayal.

"That's a very generous interpretation," she said finally, her voice low. "Sometimes I feel like I'm just stumbling around, making it up as I go along."

"Aren't we all?" Will smiled gently. "There's no map for after setbacks. You just keep moving forward, one step at a time."

They had moved slightly apart from the main crowd, standing in a quiet corner of the tent where Edwina's historical display created a sense of privacy. Around them, the sounds of the festival continued—music, laughter, announcements—but in that moment, Will was aware only of Beth's proximity, of the subtle floral scent of her perfume, of the way her eyes held his with new openness.

Later, Will wouldn't be able to say who moved first. Perhaps they both did, drawn together by the culmination of months of growing connection, of shared work and quiet conversations, of trust gradually built and walls carefully lowered. One moment they were standing close, the next, his hands were gently framing her face, and their lips were meeting in a kiss.

Beth's lips were soft against his, her hands coming to rest lightly on his chest as she leaned into the kiss. It was gentle, questioning at first, then deepening as she responded to him with unexpected ardour. Will felt a surge of emotion—tenderness, desire, and love for this woman who had come to mean so much to him.

When they finally parted, Beth's eyes were wide, a mixture of wonder and something like fear in their depths. Will kept his hands gently cradling her face, giving her time to process what had just happened.

"I've been wanting to do that since the wedding," he admitted softly. "Maybe even before."

Beth's lips curved in a small, almost shy smile. "I think I have, too," she whispered. "I just wasn't ready to admit it." Something shifted in her expression—a shadow of doubt, of reservation crossing her features. She took a small step back, not completely away but creating a slight distance between them.

"Will, I—" she began, her voice uncertain.

"It's okay," he interrupted gently, letting his hands fall to his sides. "We don't have to figure everything out right now."

Relief and gratitude flickered across her face, but the doubt remained. "It's not that I don't... feel something for you," she said carefully. "It's just—"

"Complicated," Will finished for her. "I

know. And I'm not asking for promises or declarations, Beth. Just... for you to be open to possibilities."

"I can manage that," she said with a tentative smile.

Before Will could respond, an announcement over the public address system broke the moment—something about the evening's entertainment beginning in fifteen minutes. Around them, the crowd in the tent was shifting, moving toward the exit.

"I should probably check on the students before the evening program," Beth said, professional responsibilities providing a safe retreat from emotional complexity. "Some of them are performing with the community band later."

"Of course," Will agreed, recognising her need for space to process what had happened between them. "I need to help dismantle the SES float anyway. But I'll see you tomorrow? At the dress rehearsal?"

Beth nodded, her expression warming again. "Yes. I'd like that."

When they parted near the performance area, Beth hesitated just briefly before stretching up to press a quick, soft kiss to Will's cheek. "Thank you," she murmured. "For understanding."

Then she was gone, moving through the crowd toward where her students were gathering for the evening program. Will watched her go, touching his cheek.

Was her hesitation the lingering effects of betrayal and undermined confidence? Or was it because maybe she wondered if he was the right choice?

Whatever the reasons, Will knew that pushing her would only cause Beth to retreat further. She needed space and time to process her feelings, and he was prepared to give her that time. He didn't care how long it took.

That kiss had given him hope.

The play's opening night was coming up on Wednesday, followed by the final weekend of festival events. These shared responsibilities would keep them in each other's company. And he knew he'd have to be content with that.

Small steps.

Chapter Fifteen

Beth woke before dawn, the memory of yesterday's kiss pulling her immediately from sleep into full consciousness. She lay still in the pre-dawn darkness, fingers lightly touching her lips as if searching for physical evidence of what had happened between her and Will.

He had kissed her. Or perhaps she had kissed him. And it had been... wonderful. His hands gently cradling her face, his lips warm and tender against hers, the solid strength of him as she leaned into the kiss. She'd felt safe and cherished.

But then her fear had returned—and she'd pulled back, created distance between them.

And Will had understood. Had given her space without pressure.

Beth pressed her hands to her face, overwhelmed by conflicting emotions. Desire for Will, for the warmth and acceptance she'd found in his arms. Fear of being vulnerable again, of mistaking her feelings or misjudging his intentions. Hope that this connection might be something lasting. Anxiety about the complications it created for her plans.

For months, she'd been telling herself that Bindarra Creek was temporary—a safe haven to rebuild her professional reputation before moving on to larger opportunities elsewhere. But increasingly, she found herself imagining a future here, envisioning herself as part of this community beyond the current school year. And Will was central to those imaginings, his steady presence like an anchor in her previously unmoored life.

The first hints of dawn were lightening the sky when Beth finally rose, her mind still full of Will and the kiss they'd shared. Today would be busy with final dress rehearsals for the Christmas play, leaving little time to think. But tonight, at the Carols by Candlelight event in Lette Park, she would see him again.

The thought brought both anticipation and anxiety. What if things became awkward between them? What if the ease of their friendship was lost in the complications of romance? What if she opened up, only to be hurt again?

Beth pushed her worries away. The play and

her students needed her full attention now.

The school hall was buzzing with energy when she arrived, students in various stages of costume and makeup, props and set pieces arranged for quick scene changes. Billy Kendall-Cummings was running through vocal warm-ups in one corner, while Kaylee Miller stretched in another, preparing for her dance sequence as the Ghost of Christmas Past.

"Ms Curtis!" Eddie Taylor called, hurrying over with a concerned expression. "The backing track for 'Six White Boomers' keeps skipping at the two-minute mark. I've tried cleaning the disc, but it's still happening."

Beth set her bag down, slipping immediately into professional mode. "Let's do a live accompaniment instead," she decided. "I'll play piano for that number. Can you let the others know?"

Eddie nodded and dashed off to inform the other cast members, while Beth moved to the piano to review the score. Focusing on practical problems was a relief, a welcome distraction.

For the next three hours, Beth immersed herself completely in the dress rehearsal. She addressed technical issues, fine-tuned performances, and made last-minute adjustments to staging. The students responded to her guidance with enthusiasm and commitment, their excitement about Wednesday's opening night infectious.

As they worked through the final scene, with Billy delivering Scrooge's redemption monologue against the backdrop of Will's beautifully crafted set, Beth was proud of what they had created together. From her initial reluctance to direct the play, she had come to love this project and the connection with students and community.

"That's a wrap, everyone! You are all fabulous!" she called as the final notes of the closing song faded. "You've done incredible work today. Remember, tomorrow is a day off to rest your voices. I'll see you all on Wednesday afternoon for final preparations before opening night."

As the students gathered their belongings, buzzing with excitement and nervous energy, Beth felt a hand on her shoulder. She turned to find Jaclyn Rossiter beside her, the principal's expression warm with approval.

"That was remarkable, Beth," Jackie said. "I

knew you'd do a good job with the play, but this exceeds all expectations. The colonial Christmas scene in particular—it is wonderful."

"I had good help with research." She smiled, thinking of her visit to Will's farm

Jackie's eyes twinkled knowingly. "Yes, I've heard about your research assistant. Will Greaves is quite the local historian, among his many talents."

Beth's cheeks heated, wondering if news of that kiss had somehow already spread through town; she wouldn't be at all surprised. But Jaclyn merely squeezed her shoulder before moving on to congratulate the students.

Once the hall had emptied, Beth sat at the piano, idly playing fragments of the play's musical themes as she reflected on how far they'd come since the first auditions. Will's sets had brought visual richness to each scene, placing the performance in a distinctly Australian context.

Will. Her thoughts kept circling back to him. To the way his eyes had held hers afterwards, patient and understanding even as she pulled away. To the gentle press of her lips against his cheek when they'd parted, an acknowledgment of something she wasn't yet ready to name.

Beth closed the piano lid with a decisive movement. Sitting here dwelling on yesterday wouldn't help her sort through her tangled emotions. She needed space, perspective, and time to think clearly about what she truly wanted. But if she was honest, she already knew.

***

The Carols by Candlelight event in Lette Park was scheduled for six-thirty, and she'd organised to meet the choir members at six-fifteen.

When Beth arrived at the park just after six, the area was already filling with families and groups of friends. Lette Park, named for one of the town's founding families, was a green oasis at the heart of Bindarra Creek, with ancient eucalyptus trees providing shade during the day and a sense of sheltered intimacy in the evening. For tonight's event, the central area had been arranged with concentric circles of chairs facing a small stage, while food vendors set up around the perimeter.

Beth quickly spotted her choir members gathering near the side of the stage—a mix of her school students and several parents who had joined the group over the past weeks. Will was among them, chatting easily with young Tommy Henderson and his mother, Sarah. The sight of him with the children, relaxed and encouraging, made something warm unfurl in Beth's chest.

"Miss Curtis!" called out Emma, one of her Year Seven students, waving excitedly. "We're all here!"

Beth made her way over to the group, doing a quick headcount. Fifteen voices in total—not large, but what they lacked in numbers, they made up for in enthusiasm and weeks of practice.

"Right, everyone," Beth said, gathering them in a circle. "You all know the program— 'Silent Night,' 'Carol of the Birds,' 'The Holly and the Ivy,' and finishing with 'Joy to the World.' Remember what we practised about projection and breathing."

"And watching Miss Curtis for the cues," Will added, earning nods from the younger singers.

"Exactly. Will, you're anchoring the bass line beautifully—don't be afraid to let your voice carry tonight."

As the event began, her usual pre-performance nerves kicked in, but they were tempered by confidence in her singers. The weeks of practice in the school hall, the extra sessions some of the parents had attended, all led to this moment.

When their time came, Beth positioned herself where the choir could see her clearly while still being visible to the audience. The opening notes of 'Silent Night' rose into the crisp evening air, and Beth felt immediate pride as the voices blended seamlessly. Will's bass line provided the perfect foundation, steady and warm, while the children's voices soared above.

'Carol of the Birds' showcased the arrangement Beth had adapted for their group, with Emma taking a brief solo that drew appreciative murmurs from the crowd. But it was 'The Holly and the Ivy' that truly shone—the harmony between adult and children's voices creating something magical in the starlit setting. The applause was deafening.

Their final number, 'Joy to the World,' had the entire audience joining in by the second verse, hundreds of voices united under the stars.

As the last note faded, the applause was enthusiastic and sustained, with many people calling out "Wonderful!" and "Beautiful!"

As the choir dispersed back to their families, deep satisfaction filled Beth. Months of work had culminated in this perfect moment—her students confident and proud, the community responding with genuine warmth.

"That was incredible," Will said, appearing at her side as she packed away her music folder. "Absolutely incredible, Beth."

"The children were wonderful," she replied, glowing with pride. "And the parents—they committed to the extra practice sessions. And you? You, Will, were fabulous."

"Your voice held it all together," Will said seriously. "The way you anchored the harmonies, guided them through the tempo changes in 'Carol of the Birds'—you should do more with your talent."

Beth looked up at him, surprised by the intensity in his voice. "What do you mean?"

"Performing, arranging, maybe even composing. You have a gift, Beth. Tonight proved that."

"If I had someone to push me," she said

softly, then caught herself, heat rising in her cheeks at the admission.

Will's eyes met hers, understanding passing between them. "Well," he said with a gentle smile, "consider yourself pushed."

"I should help pack up the music stands," Beth said, though she made no move to step away.

"And I should check that Tommy Henderson hasn't lost his torch again," Will replied, equally reluctant to break the connection.

They worked together in comfortable companionship, helping families gather their belongings and fold chairs. As the park gradually emptied, Beth walked beside Will toward the car park, their hands brushing occasionally in the darkness.

"Thank you," she said as they reached her car, "for being part of this. For encouraging the children, for keeping that bass line so steady."

"Thank you for including me," Will replied. "I haven't sung in a group since school. I'd forgotten how good it feels."

Beth smiled, unlocking her car. "Maybe we'll have to do it again sometime."

"I'd like that," Will said simply.

Chapter Sixteen

Will adjusted the final beam of the colonial veranda set, tightening the support bracket to ensure it would remain stable throughout the play's performances. Around him, the school hall bustled with activity—students arranging props, adjusting costumes, and running through last-minute vocal warm-ups. Opening night was less than twenty-four hours away, and the excitement was building.

From his position on the stage, Will had a perfect view of Beth as she worked with the student orchestra, fine-tuning the musical cues for each scene transition. She moved with quiet confidence among the young musicians, offering gentle corrections and encouragement in equal measure. The transformation in her since those first weeks in Bindarra was remarkable—from the hesitant newcomer wary of public performance to this assured director bringing together dozens of students in a complex production.

A surge of pride flooded through him as he

watched, knowing how much courage it had taken for Beth to embrace this role after her ex's systematic undermining of her confidence.

"Mr. Greaves?" Billy Kendall-Cummings appeared at Will's side, already in partial costume for his role as Scrooge. "Ms Curtis asked if you could check the beach scene backdrop next. There's a bit of wobble when Gavin makes his entrance as the Ghost of Christmas Present."

"I'll take care of it," Will assured him, gathering his tools. "How are you feeling about tomorrow night? Ready for your big performance?"

Billy's expression was a mixture of excitement and nervousness. "I think so. Ms Curtis has been brilliant—she showed me how to find Scrooge's humanity beneath all the meanness. Makes the character feel real, you know?"

Will nodded, impressed by the young man's insight. "That's what makes a performance memorable."

"That's exactly what Ms. Curtis says," Billy grinned. "She's the best teacher we've ever had. Everyone says so."

Will had heard similar sentiments from parents at the SES meetings, from Jaclyn Rossiter in town, from Claire McGregor, whose daughter, Megan, was having piano lessons with Beth.

Will was sure that Beth didn't realise the impact she had made in the town, in the school and her students' lives.

In just a few months, she had gone from being 'the new teacher from Sydney' to a valued and loved member of the Bindarra Creek community. She'd brought fresh approaches to the school's music programme, revitalised the Christmas play, and created innovative arrangements for the carol singers. More than that, she'd connected with students, parents, and community members on a personal level, forming relationships that went far beyond her professional role.

The thought warmed Will as he adjusted the supporting frame of the beach backdrop. Beth might still be uncertain about her future in Bindarra, might still be wary of fully embracing the personal connection developing between them, but her roots in the community were growing deeper by the day, whether she fully recognised it or not.

He secured the backdrop. "Is that better?" he called to Beth.

She looked up from her score sheets, tucking a strand of curls behind her ear in a gesture he'd come to find endearing. "Let's test it. Gavin, can you make your entrance, please? The usual vigour—don't hold back." She grinned at Will; Gavin never held back.

The innkeeper bounded onto the stage with exuberant energy, causing the backdrop to sway slightly, but it remained securely in place.

"Perfect," Beth declared, flashing Will a grateful smile that sent warmth spreading through his chest. "Thank you."

Will's phone buzzed in his pocket, breaking the moment. A text from Jon: **Don't forget *Polar Express* screening tonight at seven. Bringing Cleo and the kids.**

The reminder brought a smile to Will's face. He'd invited Beth to the special screening days ago, before their kiss, before their stargazing conversation. She'd accepted readily, mentioning that the classic film had been a childhood favourite. With all that had happened since, Will wasn't sure if their plans remained unchanged or if she might prefer some space.

As if reading his mind, Beth walked over. "We're still on for the film tonight?"

"If you'd like to be," Will replied, careful to give her an easy out if needed.

"I would," Beth said with a decisive nod that relieved his uncertainty. "I could use a break from play preparations, to be honest. Clear my head before tomorrow's opening night."

"Perfect," Will smiled. "Will I pick you up at six-thirty? The screening starts at seven, but there might be a queue for good seats."

"Six-thirty works," Beth agreed. "Though I should warn you, I cry every time the boy can't hear the bell anymore. It's embarrassing."

Will chuckled. "Your secret is safe with me. I get something in my eye during that scene, too."

Beth's answering laugh was unguarded, and her smile was wide as she went back over to the students.

By five o'clock, everything was prepared for tomorrow's opening night, and the students were released with strict instructions to rest their voices and get adequate sleep.

"It's really happening," Beth said as they

walked together to the car park after locking up the hall. "After all these weeks of preparation, they're actually going to perform for an audience tomorrow."

"They're ready," Will assured her.

"They've worked hard. And your sets make all the difference—they give the scenes an authenticity I couldn't have achieved otherwise."

"That's what community productions are all about," Will said. "I'll race home for a shower and see you at six-thirty? Warm clothes recommended—the cinema's heating is temperamental at best."

"I'll be ready," Beth promised, her eyes lingering on his for a moment before she turned towards her car.

***

The Bindarra Creek Cinema was nearly full when Will and Beth arrived, the special screening of *The Polar Express* having drawn families and film enthusiasts alike.

They found seats near the back, joining Jon and Cleo with their two young children, Benny and Charlotte.

As the lights dimmed and the film began,

Will was acutely aware of Beth beside him—her nearness, her perfume, the occasional brush of her arm against his as they shared popcorn.

True to her warning, Beth grew misty-eyed during the scene when the boy could no longer hear the bell. Without drawing attention to her emotion, Will simply offered his handkerchief, receiving a grateful smile in return. The small exchange felt significant somehow—Beth allowing herself to be vulnerable in his presence, accepting his quiet support without embarrassment.

After the film, they declined Jon and Cleo's invitation for coffee, both aware of the busy day ahead with the play's opening night. The evening air was cool as they left the cinema, the streets of Bindarra quiet in the mid-week lull.

"Would you like to come back to the cottage for tea?" Beth asked suddenly as they reached Will's ute. "I've been meaning to ask your opinion on a piece I'm working on for the finale—a new arrangement of 'Silent Night'. If you're not too tired, that is."

Will, surprised and pleased by the invitation, nodded. "I'd like that. Not tired at all."

The drive to Beth's cottage was brief. They

were quiet, both lost in their thoughts. When they arrived, Will noticed several instrument cases and sound equipment stacked near Beth's front door.

"What's all this?" he asked, gesturing to the pile.

"Equipment for tomorrow night," Beth explained. "Jaclyn arranged for some older students to help transport it to the hall, but they can't come until mid-afternoon. I was going to try to load some of it myself in the morning, but it's proving more awkward than I expected."

"I can help now, if you'd like," Will offered. "My ute's right here, and it would save you the hassle tomorrow."

Beth hesitated only briefly before nodding in gratitude. "That would be incredibly helpful. There's more inside that needs to go as well— keyboard stands, additional microphones, that sort of thing."

Together they loaded the equipment into Will's ute, working efficiently in the cool evening air.

Once the equipment was securely stowed in the vehicle, they moved inside the cottage, where Beth put the kettle on for tea. Will had been in her home only briefly before, usually just to the doorstep, and he took the opportunity to observe the space that reflected Beth.

The cottage was small but warm, with bookshelves lining one wall and a piano positioned where natural light would fall across the keys during the daytime. Sheet music was neatly arranged on a stand, and there was her collection of vinyl records that occupied a wooden crate beside a vintage turntable. The overall impression was of understated comfort; a place created for quiet reflection and creative work.

"Earl Grey or English Breakfast?" Beth called from the kitchen.

"Earl Grey, please." They settled together on the sofa, steam rising from their mugs as they sipped the hot tea. The cottage was peaceful around them, the occasional creak or settling noise only adding to the sense of cosy intimacy.

"So, this arrangement you're working on?" Will prompted after a moment.

Beth set down her mug and moved to the piano, sorting through some sheets before finding what she was looking for. "It's still very rough," she cautioned, seating herself on the bench. "I'm trying to blend the traditional melody with different rhythmic patterns. I'm not sure if it works yet."

Beth took a deep breath, fingers poised over the keys. Then, with a small nod as if confirming something to herself, she began to play.

The familiar melody of 'Silent Night' emerged, but transformed by subtle changes in rhythm and the addition of harmonies that evoked the vast Australian landscape. Beth's touch was sensitive yet confident. As she played, her body swayed slightly with the music, fully engaged in the expression of something deeply felt.

Will watched, captivated not just by the beautiful arrangement but by the transformation in Beth herself. This was Beth in her element, connected to music without self-consciousness or fear of judgment. This was the musician David had tried to silence, the artist who had been temporarily lost but was gradually finding her voice again.

When the final notes faded, Will remained silent for a moment, allowing the music to resonate in the quiet cottage. He chose his words with care. "That was extraordinary, Beth. You've captured something essential, both traditional and modern. It was beautiful."

Beth's eyes, when they met his, held a vulnerability that tugged at Will's heart. "Really? You don't think it's too experimental for the play?"

"Not at all," Will assured her. "It bridges worlds in a way that feels entirely natural. The audience will connect with it."

The tension in Beth's shoulders eased visibly at his words. "Thank you. That means a lot, especially coming from you."

"From me?" Will asked. "I'm hardly a musical expert."

"No, but you're honest," Beth said simply. "You wouldn't say you liked it just to spare my feelings. And you understand this place, this landscape, in a way I'm still learning to do. If it rings true to you, then I know I'm on the right track."

He moved to sit beside her on the piano bench, careful to maintain a respectful distance. "Would you play it again? I'd like to hear how the middle section develops."

Beth nodded, her fingers returning to the

keys with more confidence now. As she played, Will found himself watching her face more than her hands—the subtle expressions that crossed her features as she connected with the music, the occasional smile when a particular phrase pleased her, the complete absorption that transformed her from careful, guarded Beth to this fully present, expressive artist.

When she finished the second playing, she turned slightly towards him on the bench, their knees almost touching. "I'm thinking of adding a vocal line for the final verse," she said, her voice soft in the quiet room. "Something simple that the audience could join if they wanted to."

"That would be perfect," Will agreed, equally softly. "A way of bringing everyone into the experience, making it communal."

They were close now, the intimacy of sharing music having naturally drawn them toward each other. Will could see the flecks of amber in Beth's dark eyes, the curve of her lips as she smiled at his understanding, the slight flush along her cheekbones.

This time, it was Beth who moved first, leaning towards him. Will remained still, allowing her to set the pace, to make the choice that had eluded them since their interrupted kiss at the wedding. Her eyes held his, questioning and then resolving, as she closed the remaining distance between them.

Their lips had barely touched, the gentlest of contacts, when Will's phone burst into life with the distinctive ringtone reserved for SES emergencies. They jumped apart, the moment shattered by the intrusion.

"I'm sorry," Will said, genuine regret in his voice as he reached for his phone. "I have to take this."

Beth nodded understanding, moving slightly away on the bench as Will answered the call.

"Greaves," he said tersely, instantly shifting into emergency response mode.

Roman's voice was clipped and professional on the other end. "Fire reported at the western boundary, near the Taylor property. Dry lightning strike from tonight's distant storm. First response team assembling at the shed now. RFS have asked for our help."

"On my way," Will confirmed, ending the call and turning apologetically to Beth. "There's a fire out west. Likely started by lightning. I need to go."

Beth was already standing, concern evident in her expression. "Of course. Is it serious?"

"Not yet," Will assured her, gathering his keys. "But we need to contain it quickly before the wind picks up."

They moved swiftly to the door.

"Be careful," Beth said as Will prepared to leave, her voice tight with worry.

"I will," he promised. "Don't worry about the equipment in the ute—I'll make sure it gets to the hall tomorrow one way or another."

Beth shook her head, dismissing such practical concerns. "The equipment doesn't matter. Just... come back safely."

The simple statement, the naked concern in her eyes, conveyed more than elaborate declarations might have. Will reached out, briefly squeezing her hand. "I will. This is what we train for, Beth. Standard procedure."

She nodded, but the worry remained on her face as she stood in the doorway of her cottage, watching him climb into the ute. As Will drove away, headed for the SES shed and the fire beyond, he glanced in his rearview mirror to see Beth still standing there, illuminated by the porch light, one hand raised in a gesture that seemed part farewell, part prayer.

The fire glowed more distinctly on the western horizon now, a reminder of the immediate task ahead. Will pushed personal considerations aside, focusing on the emergency response procedures that were second nature after years of SES training. The fire needed to be contained, and the community needed to be protected. His feelings for Beth, their gradually deepening connection would wait.

Yet as he parked at the SES shed, where other volunteers were already donning protective gear and checking equipment, the image of Beth in her doorway stayed with him—her worried eyes, her simple plea for his safe return. Whatever happened next between them, whatever choices Beth made about her future in Bindarra and their relationship, one thing was now unmistakably clear to him: Beth cared for him. Perhaps not yet with the depth and certainty that he held, but it was a beginning.

Chapter Seventeen

Beth couldn't sleep. The distant orange glow visible from her kitchen window held her attention as she paced back and forth, checking her phone every few minutes for news. The RFS website showed the fire's location—a property on the western boundary of Bindarra Creek, uncomfortably close to several farms, including the Taylor place where Eddie, one of her students in the play, lived with his family.

She'd made tea but hadn't drunk it, and started reading but couldn't focus on the words. Her mind kept returning to Will—their kiss, the sudden emergency call, the concern in his eyes as he reassured her before leaving. The way her heart had constricted watching him drive toward danger.

By dawn, exhaustion had set in, but sleep remained elusive. Beth showered and dressed mechanically, then headed to the café far earlier than necessary, seeking information as much as caffeine.

Claire looked up as the bell jangled, her

expression weary but relieved. "You've heard about the fire, then?"

Beth nodded, approaching the counter. "Any news? Is everyone alright?"

"Under control now," Claire confirmed, pouring coffee without being asked. "Roman called Craig half an hour ago. No structures lost, though the Taylors' western paddock is pretty scorched."

"And the firefighters?" Beth asked the question she really wanted to ask—*Is Will safe?*—hovering unspoken.

Claire's smile suggested she heard the unasked question. "All safe. Exhausted, but safe. They'll be wrapping up soon."

Relief washed through Beth, so powerful she had to grasp the counter for support. "Thank goodness," she whispered.

"The opening night's still happening?" Claire asked, sliding the coffee toward her.

Beth straightened. "Absolutely. Final dress rehearsal this afternoon, performance tonight. The students have worked too hard to postpone."

Her day unfolded in a blur of activity— collecting the equipment from Will's ute at the

SES shed, coordinating last-minute details with Jac, managing the growing excitement of the student performers. Through it all, concern for Will remained a constant undercurrent, along with the memory of their newfound closeness.

By afternoon, the students were assembled in the hall for the final dress rehearsal. Beth moved among them, offering reassurance and final notes, her outward calm belying her inner distraction. As she raised her baton to begin the opening number, her gaze drifted involuntarily to the empty seat in the front row—the one Will had promised to occupy tonight.

"Focus," she murmured to herself, then louder to the students: "Places, everyone. From the top."

The rehearsal progressed smoothly, the weeks of preparation evident in the polished performances. Billy's Scrooge was perfectly calibrated between bitterness and vulnerability, Kaylee's ghostly dancing was hauntingly beautiful, and the musical numbers flowed seamlessly between scenes. Even with her divided attention, Beth could see they were ready, could feel the magic they'd created together.

Halfway through the colonial Christmas scene, Beth became aware of movement at the back of the hall. Looking up from her conductor's podium, she saw him—Will, still in his SES uniform, streaks of soot on his face, but very much whole and safe. Their eyes met across the distance, his tired smile warming something inside her that she hadn't known was cold.

Beth continued directing, her movements more relaxed now, tension draining from her shoulders with each beat of the music. Will found a seat at the back, watching without interrupting, his presence alone enough to steady her racing thoughts.

The rehearsal concluded with her new arrangement of 'Silent Night'—the piece she'd played for Will the previous evening. As the final notes approached, Beth made a spontaneous decision that would have been unthinkable months ago.

"Wait," she said, lowering her baton. "I'd like to try something different for the finale." She turned to the students, aware of Will watching from the back. "The arrangement needs a vocal line. Would you mind if I demonstrated what I'm thinking?"

The students nodded eagerly, curious about this unexpected development. Beth stepped away from the podium, positioned herself centre stage, and nodded to the pianist to begin.

And then Beth Curtis, who had not performed publicly since David's cutting criticisms had silenced her voice, began to sing.

The melody was simple but haunting, blending traditional European harmonies with rhythmic elements inspired by the land's first peoples. Beth's clear soprano filled the hall, carrying emotions she'd kept carefully contained for too long—gratitude for this community that had welcomed her, joy in creating music with these talented young people, and something deeper, more personal, directed towards the man watching silently from the back row.

When she finished, the hall remained silent for a heartbeat before erupting in spontaneous applause—students, stagehands, even Jac, who had slipped in during the rehearsal. Beth felt tears threatening, overwhelmed by the moment, by her own courage in reclaiming this part of herself.

As the students were dismissed with final instructions for the evening performance, Beth remained on stage, organising her score sheets with trembling hands. She sensed rather than heard Will's approach, his quiet footsteps on the wooden stage floor.

"That was beautiful," he said simply, his voice rough with exhaustion and emotion.

Beth turned to face him, taking in the soot smudges, the redness around his eyes from smoke exposure, the weariness in his stance. "You're safe," she whispered, the words carrying all the fear and worry of the long night.

"I promised I would be," Will replied, a small smile softening his tired features.

Beth stepped forward then, caution and hesitation falling away as she wrapped her arms around him, heedless of the ash that would transfer to her clothes. Will's arms came around her immediately, strong and secure, his cheek resting against her hair.

"I was so worried," Beth admitted against his shoulder. "I couldn't sleep, couldn't stop thinking about you out there."

Will's arms tightened slightly. "I'm alright. The fire's contained, everyone's safe."

They stood like that for a long moment, Beth listening to the steady beat of his heart, confirmation of his safety more reassuring than any words could be. When she finally pulled back, Will's eyes held a question she was finally ready to answer.

"I'm falling in love with you, Will Greaves," Beth said softly. "I've been fighting it because I'm scared. But watching you drive toward that fire last night, not knowing if you'd come back safely to me..." She shook her head, emotion closing her throat momentarily. "I couldn't bear it if something happened to you without you knowing how I feel."

Will's hands came up to gently frame her face, his eyes never leaving hers. "I've been falling for you since the day you arrived in Bindarra Creek, and I met you at the CWA meeting," he confessed. "But I would have waited as long as you needed, Beth. This is worth waiting for."

"I still have fears," Beth cautioned, honesty compelling her to acknowledge the lingering shadows from her past. "I'm still learning to trust myself again, to believe in what I feel."

"We have time," Will assured her, his

thumbs gently brushing her cheeks. "All the time we need."

This time, when their lips met, there were no interruptions, no emergency calls, no retreats. Just Beth and Will, finding each other. The kiss was gentle at first, then deepened with shared emotion—relief, joy, and the confirmation of feelings too strong to deny any longer.

When they parted, Beth smiled up at him, a new certainty settling in her heart. "You should go home and rest. You've been fighting fire all night, and I need to prepare for opening night."

"I'll be in the front row," Will promised, pressing his forehead to hers. "Wild horses couldn't keep me away."

"I know," Beth said simply, and she did know—trusted in his word, in his steady presence, in the connection they'd forged through shared work and quiet conversations, through music and under stars.

As Will left to go home and sleep, Beth remained on the stage where she'd reclaimed her confidence and her belief in herself, where she'd finally acknowledged her feelings for Will. Tonight, the play would open—her students would shine, the community would gather, and Will would be watching from the front row.

Some risks, she reflected as she gathered her things, were worth taking after all. And Will Greaves—solid, patient, perceptive Will—was perhaps the most worthwhile risk of all.

Chapter Eighteen

Will straightened his tie as he took his place in the front row of the packed school hall. Around him, the excited murmur of the crowd grew as townspeople and visitors gathered for the Christmas play's final performance, coinciding with the festival finale. The three previous nights had been successful beyond anyone's expectations, with standing-room-only crowds and enthusiastic reviews in the local paper.

Tonight's audience included not just locals but visitors from surrounding towns, drawn by word of mouth about the innovative production. Will spotted Roman and Joe with their families, and Tessa from the Fig Tree Lodge.

The lights dimmed, and a hush fell over the audience. From his vantage point, Will could see Beth in the wings, offering final words of encouragement to her students. She wore a simple but elegant cream dress, her curls arranged in a style that framed her face beautifully. Even from a distance, he could see the confidence in her posture, the calm assurance with which she directed last-minute adjustments.

What a transformation from the guarded, hesitant woman who had arrived in Bindarra Creek just a few months ago. Pride swelled in Will's chest, not because he had any claim to her accomplishments, but because he had been privileged to witness her journey—the gradual reclaiming of her voice, her talent, her joy in music.

The music began, and the curtain rose on the opening scene—Will's Victorian parlour set illuminated perfectly, Billy Kendall-Cummings transformed into a convincing Scrooge amid the period furnishings. The audience's appreciative murmur at the set's detail brought a small smile to Will's face, but his attention was primarily on Beth as she conducted the small orchestra with graceful, assured movements.

Throughout the performance, Will found himself watching her as much as the action on stage. She was fully in her element—guiding the music with subtle gestures, occasionally mouthing lines along with the actors, her face alight with pride in her students' accomplishments. This was the Beth that David had tried to diminish, the confident musician whose gifts were now benefiting an entire community.

When the final scene arrived, featuring Beth's innovative arrangement of 'Silent Night', a ripple of anticipation passed through the audience. Word had spread about this unique musical moment, blending European tradition with indigenous rhythms in a distinctly Australian reimagining of the Christmas classic.

To everyone's surprise, including Will's, Beth stepped from behind the conductor's podium and took centre stage. A moment of silence fell, broken only when she began to sing—her clear soprano filling the hall with a melody that spoke of both universal themes and the unique spirit of this land. The student choir joined harmoniously on the second verse, but it was Beth's voice that carried the emotion, strong and unafraid, reclaiming what had once been taken from her.

Will's eyes pricked with tears, and his chest tightened with emotion, remembering how she'd once told him she no longer sang, how David's criticism had silenced her public voice.

Yet here she was, singing with confidence and joy before a packed audience, her gaze occasionally finding his as if drawing strength from their connection.

When the final notes faded, there was a moment of breathless silence before the hall erupted in thunderous applause. The audience rose to their feet, cheering as Beth rejoined her students for the curtain call. The standing ovation continued as Beth gestured to the orchestra, the backstage crew, and finally—with a meaningful smile—to Will in the front row, acknowledging his contribution to the sets.

The celebration spilled into the school grounds, where refreshments had been arranged before the festival finale at Lette Park. Will made his way through the crowd, accepting congratulations on the sets while keeping an eye out for Beth among the throngs of well-wishers surrounding her and the student performers.

When he finally reached her, she was flushed with success, her eyes bright with the exhilaration of the performance.

"You were magnificent," Will said simply, resisting the urge to gather her into his arms in such a public setting. "The arrangement, your voice—everything was perfect."

"We did it," Beth replied, her smile radiant. "All of us together. I couldn't have managed any of this without the community's support. Without you."

Before Will could respond, they were surrounded by Beth's students, eager to share their excitement and relief after four successful performances. Will stepped back, content to watch as Beth celebrated with her pupils, praising individual performances and sharing in their achievement.

It was nearly an hour later when Beth found him again, now standing at the edge of the schoolyard as people began moving toward Lette Park for the festival finale.

"Walk with me to the park?" she asked, slipping her hand naturally into his.

They strolled together through the lantern-lit streets, joining the flow of townspeople and visitors heading to the culminating event of the month-long festival. Lette Park had been transformed for the occasion, with food stalls representing the cooking classes, a central bonfire, and strings of lights creating a magical canopy above the celebration.

"I want to tell you something, Will."

He took her hands and stood in front of her. "Tell me."

Beth nodded, leaning slightly into his touch. "I'm done being afraid of happiness. Done letting the past dictate my future. Whatever happens next, I want to move towards it with you, not away from it in fear."

Around them, the festival reached its peak—music playing from the central stage, families enjoying specialties from the cooking class stalls, laughter and conversation filling the cool evening air. As darkness fell completely, the promised drone light display began, with dozens of programmed drones creating shifting patterns of light high above the park.

"Dance with me?" Will asked, extending his hand as the music shifted to a slower, more romantic melody.

Beth stepped into his arms without hesitation, moving naturally with him as they had at the wedding, but now without the careful distance, without the uncertainty and retreat. Her body fit perfectly against his, her head resting comfortably on his shoulder as they swayed to the music beneath the dancing lights overhead.

"I love you, Beth Curtis," Will said quietly, the words he'd been holding back for weeks finally finding voice in this perfect moment.

Beth raised her head to meet his gaze, her eyes shining with emotion. "And I love you, Will Greaves. With all my healing heart."

Their kiss, witnessed by twinkling drones above and distant stars beyond, sealed a promise that had been forming since their first meeting—a connection built on mutual respect, on shared work and quiet understanding, on patient waiting and gradual trust.

Epilogue

One month later, Beth stood on the verandah of Will's farmhouse, watching the sun set over paddocks dotted with sheep and new lambs. The school term had begun two weeks ago, her position now confirmed for the full year ahead, with strong hints from Jaclyn about a permanent appointment next year to follow.

"Penny for your thoughts?" Will asked, joining her with two steaming mugs of tea.

"Just reflecting," Beth smiled, accepting the mug gratefully. "On everything that's changed since I arrived in Bindarra. On how different my life is from what I'd planned."

"Regrets?" Will asked, though his tone suggested he knew the answer.

"Not one," Beth assured him, leaning comfortably against his solid warmth. "How could I regret finding my voice again? Finding community? Finding you?"

Their weekend routine had developed naturally over the past month—Beth spending Saturdays and Sundays at the farm, learning about rural life, occasionally helping with the sheep, and discovering a deep connection to the land through Will's patient guidance. Her cottage in town remained her own space, a gradual transition that respected both her independence and the newness of their relationship.

"Edwina called this morning," Beth mentioned, suppressing a smile. "Asked if she should start shopping for a fascinator for spring."

Will chuckled, his arm tightening around her waist. "Subtle as ever, our Edwina."

"I told her not to rush," Beth replied, turning to face him. "But not to discard the idea either."

Will's smile was gentle. They hadn't discussed long-term plans explicitly, both content to let their relationship develop at its own pace. But Beth's casual acknowledgment of a future together represented another small step forward, another opening of her once-guarded heart.

"Come with me," Will said suddenly, taking her hand. "There's something I want to show you."

He led her to his ute, and they drove along

farm tracks as the sky deepened from gold to purple, eventually stopping at a rise overlooking the entire property. The first stars were appearing overhead, the air cool but pleasant as they walked to a fallen log positioned perfectly for watching the sunset.

"This is my thinking spot," Will explained as they sat together. "Where I come when I need perspective, when decisions need making, when the day's been too full or too empty."

Beth looked around, understanding immediately why Will treasured this place. The panoramic view of the property, the perfect quiet broken only by distant sheep and the whisper of eucalyptus leaves, the vast sky opening above them—it embodied everything she'd come to love about this land.

"It's beautiful," she said simply.

"I've never brought anyone else here," Will admitted, his voice quiet in the gathering dusk. "It's always been just mine. But I wanted to share it with you, because..." He paused, choosing his words carefully. "Because when I think about the future—about all the sunsets and seasons ahead—I see you in them, Beth. Here, with me."

The simple declaration, so characteristic of Will's straightforward honesty, moved Beth deeply. She turned to face him, taking both his hands in hers.

"I see that too," she confessed. "When I imagine my life moving forwards, you're at the centre of it. You, this place, the community we're part of."

Will's smile in the fading light was tender. "No more temporary haven? No more stepping stone to somewhere else?"

Beth shook her head, certainty filling her voice. "I'm home, Will. In Bindarra Creek. In my music. With you. I don't need to search anymore."

Under the stars, their kiss sealed their commitment to each other. A promise. A direction. A harmony composed by two hearts finding their complementary melodies.

Later, as they lay on a blanket watching the stars wheel overhead, the last lingering shadows of Beth's past faded completely. David's voice, once so cutting and intrusive in her mind, had been replaced by the sounds of Bindarra—student laughter, community singing, Will's steady heartbeat beneath her ear.

"What are you thinking now?" Will asked softly, his fingers gently playing with her hair.

Beth smiled in the darkness, the truth simple and complete. "I'm thinking about music," she said. "About how separate notes come together to create something greater than themselves. About harmony and counterpoint, tension and resolution."

"And us?" Will prompted gently as his arms tightened around her, his lips brushing her temple.

"We're finding *our* harmony," Beth replied, nestling closer against him. "Different melodies that complement each other perfectly. The music of us."

THE END

Thank you for reading my story. I hope you enjoyed Beth and Will's journey.

About the Multi-Author Bindarra Creek Christmas in July Romance Series

Welcome to Bindarra Creek, a struggling country town where people work hard and love deeply. Set in the picturesque tablelands of New England, Australia, Bindarra Creek is a fictional, rural community full of romance, intrigue, adventure, drama and suspense.

This latest series, **Bindarra Creek Christmas in July romances**, is the seventh multi-best-selling author series set in the fictional small town of Bindarra Creek. The books can be read in any order, and each book features a stand-alone romance.

Hidden Dreams – Suzanne Gilchrist

Cooking up Christmas – Susanne Bellamy

Hearts in Harmony – Annie Seaton

It Might be You – Juanita Kees

Second Chance Christmas – Kerrie Paterson

A Winter's Promise – Rhonda Forrest

About That Dance - Linda Charles

The other series are:
Bindarra Creek Small Town Christmas – released 1st December 2023
The Glitter or The Gold – Suzanne Gilchrist
Christmas at the Cyprus Café – Susanne Bellamy
A Place to Belong – Annie Seaton
A Magical Summer - Rhonda Forrest
Destined to Stay – Kerrie Paterson
Home for Christmas – Lauren K McKellar
The Christmas Surprise – Linda Charles
The Gift of Bindarra Creek – Lindsay Douglas

A Bindarra Creek Christmas Romance 2022
The Mistletoe Wish – Suzanne Gilchrist
The Christmas Jinx – Susanne Bellamy
The Grinch of Bindarra Creek – Lindsay Douglas
Christmas at Forrest Glen - Rhonda Forrest
Mistletoe Magic – Erin Moira O'Hara
Mistletoe and Blue Jeans – Linda Charles
A Clever Christmas – Annie Seaton
Tangled by Tinsel – Phillipa Nefri Clark
A Cowboy for Christmas – Lauren K McKellar

A Bindarra Creek Mystery Romance
A Dangerous Secret – Suzanne Gilchrist
Beyond the Gate – Rhonda Forrest
Protecting their Destiny – Erin Moira O'Hara
Only She Knew – Linda Charles
Secrets of River Cottage – Annie Seaton
Forgotten Secrets – Susanne Bellamy
A Perfect Danger – Phillipa Nefri Clark

Bindarra Creek: A Town Reborn
Take Me Home – Suzanne Gilchrist
In the Heat of the Night – Susanne Bellamy
No Looking Back - Linda Charles
Worth the Wait – Annie Seaton
With Every Breath – Lauren K. McKellar
Stealing Her Heart – Simone Angela
A Twist of Fate – Erin Moira O'Hara
Promise Me Forever – Juanita Kees

Bindarra Creek Short & Sweet
What's in a Kiss – Linda Charles
My Forever Valentine – Sandie James
Pearls and Green Beer – Susanne Bellamy
Full Circle – Annie Seaton
Date with Destiny – Erin Moira O'Hara
A Letter From the Queen – Lee Christine

Love's Sweet Challenge – Suzanne Gilchrist
The Widow Maker – Lauren K. McKellar
Out of the Blue – Noelle Clark

Bindarra Creek Romance
Bindarra Creek Makeover - Suzanne Gilchrist
Shadows of the Heart- Lee Christine
Second Chance Love - Susanne Bellamy
The CEO Mechanic - Sandie James
Reach for the Stars - Kerrie Paterson
Home to Bindarra Creek - Juanita Kees
Stolen Sanctuary - Stacey Nash
Tempting Fate - Erin Moira O'Hara
One More Day - Linda Charles
The Vine - Lauren K. McKellar
The Ghost of His Past - Simone Angela
Joanie's Dilemma - Marianne Theresa
Buckley's Chance - Noelle Clark

Full details on buy links for all books in the Bindarra Creek world can be found at:
www.bindarracreekromance.com

Also by Annie Seaton
Daughters of the Darling
From Across the Sea
Over the River
By the Billabong
Beneath Still Waters

A Bec Whitfield Mystery
Bowen River
Shadows on the Shore
Storm Season

Duckinwilla Days
Coming Home
Secrets and Surprises
Wishes and Whispers
Chasing Dreams
New Beginnings

The Enchanted Village series
A Magic Christmas

Home to the Outback
Lucy
Angie
Jemima
Isabella
Porter Sisters Series
Kakadu Sunset
Daintree
Diamond Sky
Hidden Valley
Larapinta
Kakadu Dawn

Others
Whitsunday Dawn
Undara
Osprey Reef
East of Alice
One Summer in Tuscany
Four Seasons Short and Sweet
Follow the Sun
Ten Days in Paradise
Deadly Secrets
Adventures in Time
Silver Valley Witch
The Emerald Necklace

ANNIE SEATON

A Clever Christmas
Christmas with the Boss
Her Christmas Star
The Emerald Necklace

The Augathella Girls Series
Outback Roads
Outback Sky
Outback Escape
Outback Wind
Outback Dawn
Outback Moonlight
Outback Dust
Outback Hope
Boxed Sets
Augathella Girls 1-4
Augathella Girls 5-8

Augathella Short and Sweet Series
An Augathella Surprise
An Augathella Baby
An Augathella Spring
An Augathella Christmas
An Augathella Wedding
An Augathella Easter

HEARTS IN HARMONY

An Augathella Masquerade Ball
Boxed Set
Augathella Short and Sweet 1-3
Augathella Short and Sweet 1-4

Sunshine Coast Series
Waiting for Ana
The Trouble with Jack
Healing His Heart
Sunshine Coast Boxed Set

The Richards Brothers Series
The Trouble with Paradise
Marry in Haste
Outback Sunrise
Richards Brothers Boxed Set

Bondi Beach Love Series
Beach House
Beach Music
Beach Walk
Beach Dreams
The House on the Hill Boxed Set

Second Chance Bay Series
Her Outback Playboy

Her Outback Protector
Her Outback Haven
Her Outback Paradise
Boxed Set
The McDougalls of Second Chance Bay Set

Love Across Time Series
Come Back to Me
Follow Me
Finding Home
The Threads that Bind
Boxed Set
Love Across Time 1-4

Bindarra Creek Books
Worth the Wait
Full Circle
Secrets of River Cottage
A Clever Christmas
A Place to Belong
Hearts in Harmony

Awards

2025: Finalist- Romantic Suspense category - RUBY award -*From Across the Sea*

2023: Winner - Long contemporary novel category, RUBY award -*Larapinta.*

2023*:* Finalist - Australian Romance Readers Awards- *Kakadu Dawn,* the sixth and final book in the Porter Sisters series.

2018 and 2020: Finalist - for the NZ KORU Award.

2017: Winner - Best Established Author of the Year 2017 AUSROM

2017: Winner - Author of the Year, 2014 AUSROM
 Best Established Author, AUSROM Readers' Choice.

2016, 2017, 2018, 2019: Longlisted - Sisters in Crime Davitt Awards

2016: Finalist - Book of the Year, Long Romance, RWA Ruby Awards for *Kakadu Sunset*

2015: Winner - Best Established Author of the Year AUSROM

About the Author

Annie Seaton lives near the beach on the mid-north coast of New South Wales. Her career and studies spanned the education sector, including working as an academic research librarian, a high-school principal and a university tutor until she took early retirement and fulfilled her lifelong dream of a full-time writing career.

Each winter, Annie and her husband leave the beach to roam the remote areas of Australia for story ideas and research. She is passionate about preserving the beauty of the Australian landscape and respecting the traditional ownership of the land. For those readers who cannot experience this journey personally, Annie seeks to portray the natural beauty of the Australian environment—its spiritual locations, stunning landscapes and unique wildlife.

Readers can contact Annie through her website, annieseaton.net, or find her on

Facebook and Instagram.